Ted's Tales Two

Ted Delgrosso

ISBN: 978-1-962624-16-9

Dedication

To my family, my reason for everything.

Preface

Tell Me A Story

It all started when I was a little boy.

When my parents brought my younger brother Jimmy and me to our grandparents' house in western New Jersey, we would all enjoy the day or the weekend in a much different way than at home. They lived in a rural setting with more woods and fields than neighbors, and this allowed Jimmy and I to experience nature much more than in our own grassy backyard. Exploring our grandparents' two-acre property gave us much insight into the natural world.

And it did not end there. During the afternoon, especially if rain kept us inside, we would ask our grandfather to tell us a story, and he did. My brother and I would sit on the floor in front of his chair as he would tell his tales. Grandpa would always start out by pointing to something in the living room where we all sat or refer to something else in a house filled with interesting things.

There was an antelope display on the wall above the television set. In one of his first stories to us, Grandpa spoke of his trip to Wyoming one year in the 1950s when he and two friends took a guided hunt for the fast-running animal, of how he had practiced long-range shooting for weeks before they left and how he learned the hard way how good an antelope's vision is. Success came after two failed attempts to get within range, but in the end, he prevailed.

The *"tell me a story"* part of the many visits to our grandparents' house had a huge influence on me as I grew older. Early on, as our parents were driving us home, I even asked Dad, who was a fireman, and Mom, who was the homemaker for our family, to share their stories. Most of the time, we would hear interesting tales of their lives, how they thought about things, and the experiences they had.

Mom told us about her labor of love as she prepared for Thanksgiving, a very big deal in our house. We were not allowed in the dining room from Monday to Thanksgiving Day, and we never knew why until Mom told us her tale. She explained everything, from cleaning the room from floor to ceiling, taking the fancy serving set out of the hutch, doing all the cooking and preparation all the way through to the five separate sittings at the table on Thanksgiving itself.

As I went through my teen years, I tried to make it a point to ask people I encountered to tell me a story, anything they wanted. Most who did so told their tales in unorganized, choppy ways, and I had to think a lot to get the meaning of what they were saying. Some, however, displayed well-organized, well-sequenced orations filled with details and actions that made their stories come alive and were quite interesting.

And so, as I decided to become a storyteller myself, I followed the best examples I had heard from others. I thought about what I wanted to say, organized a logical progression, and practiced telling the stories out loud to myself and to captive audiences like our cat Jingles *(no feedback there)*. Jimmy suffered through many of my rehearsals but did give me an opportunity to refine my craft. At first, when my parents heard me wandering around the house mumbling to myself, they thought I was crazy, but then approved once I explained the what and the why.

As for the why, while in the Boy Scouts, my troop did a lot of camping, and I had many opportunities to peddle my wares around the campfire at night. This expanded to party situations and any time I was with others waiting for something or other. I would usually invite someone else to tell a story first and then take my turn. I learned that storytelling is an art form with a rich history. It must be learned, improved upon, rehearsed, and, above all else, enjoyed. The joy in telling often allows an audience some level of joy in listening. I have found this art to be a device that serves to bring friends and even strangers together in a positive way, if only for a few minutes. It is a good thing.

Now that I am more of a writer, I try to bring all these storytelling factors to my written work. Besides telling stories, I have been writing stories for many years and am now a published author. Writing does not allow any do-overs as the reader reads the piece, so all the elements need to be in place once the final rewrite is submitted. A different challenge for sure, but one I embrace with all my heart.

Table Of Contents

Dedication	3
Preface	4
Part One: Contemporary Fiction	**9**
Close Call	10
Tall	14
Interview: Fireman	20
Blown Away	26
The Competition	30
Right Off the Bat	34
The Man at the Door	40
Proceed and Persist	45
Pheasanting	48
Today's the Day	56
Sniper Thoughts	61
Full Circle	64
Swim Call	66
Cousins	72
Porch Chair	76
Part Two: Science Fiction	**84**
Traveling Through Torrey Pines	85
The Rock	94
The White Lady	99
Felony Stop	106

Yearbook	110
Sharing	117
The Offer	123
Our Blue Book	126
Skin	138
Henry Oak	147
Charon's Surprise	153
Hi Mickey!	160
Swimming on Ence	170
Uptown Girl	177
The Carnival	181
Acknowledgment	187
About the Author	188

Part One:
Contemporary Fiction

Close Call

My cousin Raymond lives in a cabin up in Maine, not far from Long Pond, a remote lake in the middle of a vast forest. He is part of a small community that values independence above all other things. He lives a simple life but is quite happy with it.

While visiting with Ray last summer, I had an occasion where I took a hike along one of the trails that passed by his property. Ray couldn't join me that day but made sure I armed myself with a handgun before I departed. We mapped out the area, and he told me my hike would take about three hours. I left after breakfast.

Walking through the woods in Maine is a lot different than the hikes I was used to taking in New Jersey. There, you were never too far from civilization in case of an emergency, as the state is densely populated, even in the outlying areas. But here, in Maine, it is true wilderness. And the wildlife up here is a lot more unpredictable. Coyotes, black bears, and even wolves roam here, hence the firearm.

After about an hour on the trail, I broke the cover of the woods and found myself on a lakefront beach. It was a clearing just off Long Pond that was mostly sandy soil and loose rocks. Several pieces of driftwood lay about, and I saw an old fisherman's net entangled in one of them. It looked like it had been there for some time since part of it was buried in the sand.

It was then I noticed a movement in the net. As I approached, I discovered a small dog, not more than a puppy, caught up in the net. It was hopelessly ensnared and, from its weak motion, was near exhaustion. Getting closer, I saw that this was not a domesticated dog. Its fur was rough and matted. It had no collar and looked wild. It looked mostly like a German Shepherd with a bit of Pit Bull mixed in. When it noticed me, the puppy showed its teeth and tried to growl, but I felt pity rather than fear.

I squatted down next to the puppy, careful to approach it from the rear to avoid its teeth, and saw that part of the net had cut into his left ear, deep enough to cause bleeding, though now dried up. I therefore named the puppy *"Clefty"* in my mind.

I took out my knife and, moving slowly, started to cut through the netting that had entangled Clefty's rear legs. Though the netting parted quickly, I took my time as I wanted to ensure that it did not appear threatening. Clefty was a bit restless at first but soon relaxed and settled down.

Finally, I reached the point where I had to clear the area around his head. Here, the netting was at its worst as it was layered quite thickly around Clefty's head. Poor dog. He must have struggled for some time, only to get more and more entangled. I moved slowly, from the back, to both avoid his teeth and to also be careful not to cut my new friend. Clefty seemed to know somehow that I meant no harm and remained still as I worked. I was especially careful around his eyes and snout, and the last thing I did was lift the net out of his injured ear.

Finally free, the puppy stood up and slowly started to walk toward the woods, shaky on his feet.

It was only then that I noticed what had to be Clefty's mother. It was a full-grown version of the puppy itself, with mangy hair, long ears, and that same feral look. Next to her were two other puppies, most likely Clefty's siblings. But what I noticed most of all were her eyes, fixed on me. I realized she had been watching me the entire time from when I first came onto the lakeshore, just watching.

I stood up very slowly at this point and backed up a step, keeping my eyes steady on hers. Clefty, during this time, was slowly making his way back to the mother. Her eyes quickly looked at him, only to snap back to me less than a second later.

Then I saw another adult dog in the woods, behind and off to the side, closer to me than the mother. A quick scan revealed two others in the woods, now forming a crescent around me. I realized then that I was in a bit of trouble, surrounded by a pack of wild dogs. There were probably other members of the pack that I had not seen, and they were all now focused on me.

I was terrified but knew I couldn't show it. At this point, as I looked back at the mother, I saw that Clefty had just about reached her. She stepped forward and lowered her head toward the pup. She gave Clefty a few short licks, then raised her head and once again looked at me. I remained frozen, knife still in hand and gun still at my hip, but I had no idea what was coming.

The mother continued to look at me and started a slow walk toward me along the sand. I knew that running away or even stepping back again would trigger a chase response, so I just remained still even as she continued her approach.

What happened next was amazing. The mother, a hulking wild dog that must have weighed nearly a hundred pounds, came within five feet of me. In desperation, I stuck my left hand out toward her, the one without the knife, and offered it to her, fingers down, half expecting it to be bitten. But instead, she slowly closed the remaining space between us and licked my hand, not once but twice. Her eyes then held mine for a moment, and then, very quickly, she turned and went back to her pups.

As startled by this as I was, I also felt enormous relief. It was clear that I had been thanked by a feral dog, probably the alpha of a pack of wild dogs. The fact that this had happened, as opposed to me being torn to shreds, was a miracle. And I was grateful.

But just as I was celebrating, the final act took place. The mother, after moving her three pups back into the woods, started to follow them. But before the mother herself disappeared into the thickets, she turned once more to me, and as our eyes met for the last time, she bared her teeth and growled at me in a threatening manner. Then she was gone, and as I looked around, all the other dogs departed as well.

Walking back to the cabin, my hike now over, I considered all that had happened. I could have fired the pistol into the air in the hope that it may have scared the dogs away. But, given the strong maternal instincts of the mother, it could have had the opposite effect, triggering aggression by the entire pack. That would have quickly overwhelmed any of my abilities. So, in a world of uncertainty, what actually occurred turned out to be the best outcome for all involved. The fact that my actions to save the puppy ended up saving my own life will never be lost on me. Kindness begets kindness, sometimes even across different species.

Tall

"Land ho!" shouted Genaro from the crow's nest. "Two points off the starboard bow." He had found an island, once again proving his value to the ship.

Genaro Mastroianni was a crewman on a ship in the days of wood and sail. He lived a better-than-average life in a coastal home just south of the wharves of San Francisco. His wife and children enjoyed a life of riches far beyond the average family of the day and even had a few servants to take care of their needs. This was all because Genaro had a special gift: his extraordinary eyesight. He could see clearer and further than most people and even bested some with a spyglass. This made him quite valuable to all of the sea captains, and there was great competition for his services as a lookout. As a result, he was always given an officer's status on board a ship and a very large share of the ship's profits.

On this particular cruise, Genaro was on the Marybelle, a three-masted clipper that had gone to the South Pacific to secure a cargo of vegetable oils, coconuts, and spices. Such journeys, though profitable in the end, were fraught with dangers. Violent storms at sea could sink a ship of the day very quickly. An attack at sea by ships of other nations or even pirates was a real possibility. However, the threat that challenged

Marybelle at this time was the lack of critical supplies, water, and fresh fruits. Fresh water, in particular, was running low, and it became essential that they make landfall anywhere to replenish.

It wasn't long before the ship lay at anchor offshore, and a small boat was launched. The boat carried seven men and a quantity of empty water barrels and burlap sacks. Each man was armed with a pistol and the makings of five shots, as it was known that many of these islands hosted hostile natives. Shortly after landing the boat, they quickly disappeared into the jungle that bordered the small, sandy beach.

Several hours passed before Genaro spotted a lone sailor as he stumbled back out of the forest, took a few steps onto the sand, and fell down face-first onto the beach. Genaro notified the captain, and shortly afterward, another boat was launched to rescue the man, this time with Genaro aboard.

When they finally got to Kacy, the fallen man, he was barely alive. As two others held him up to a sitting position, Genaro gave Kacy a drink of water and drew near to him as it became apparent Kacy was trying to speak. As Genaro put his ear close to the man's mouth, he heard Kacy utter one word, "tall," and then he fell over, dead. Since there was no sign of any other crewmen, the officer in charge ordered the sailors to recover the other boat and bring both back to the Marybelle.

Once aboard, Kacy was brought below and examined by the doctor. Besides a small scratch on the sailor's neck, there was no sign of any injury that would have caused his death. But since the area around the scratch was dark and swollen, the doctor reported to the captain that he suspected Kacy had been killed by a poison arrow or something similar that had given him a grazing hit.

In other circumstances, especially with the assumed loss of six crewmen and an officer, the captain would have ordered that the Marybelle hoist anchor and return to sea, but their emergency had become serious enough to warrant another expedition. And so, this time, two boats were dispatched. One team was to follow the path of the original expedition and attempt to locate the other sailors as well as seek out a water source. The other boat would follow along the shoreline for a while before making landfall. At that time, the sailors would disembark and walk along the beach, hoping to find a river or stream of fresh water as it emptied into the sea. Genaro was to accompany the first team. It was hoped that he would spot any trouble before it was too late.

Soon after, the boat carrying Genaro, second mate Clifton, and five others made landfall close to where the first expedition had landed.

"I want you two, Womack and Samuelson, to keep an eye on Genaro here as we try to find out what happened to the other fellows," Mr. Clifton ordered. "Maple, you are with me. And Nelson and Collins take the lead. If you see anything strange, stop, and we will send Genaro up to take a closer look."

With that, the group pushed into the jungle.

They moved slowly along a path that showed the footprints of the earlier expedition. The going was challenging as the jungle was thick all around them, and the path was narrow. After about an hour, the growth thinned out a little, and finally, up ahead, they could see a clearing.

No sooner had they arrived at the edge of the clearing than Maple signaled them to stop. Mr. Clifton was told that there were some of the crewmen up ahead, their bodies laid out on the ground near the far side of the clearing, where, once again, the trail led off into the jungle. As planned, Genaro was then brought up front to the tree line. He found a high spot in the terrain from which he had a clear view of the field ahead as well as the beginnings of the jungle beyond. He stood very still and slowly scanned what lay before him.

He immediately saw several of their fellow crewmen strung out along the ground. All seemed almost in a straight line, as if they had all fallen at nearly the same time. The line of bodies started about twenty yards from the far end of the clearing and extended into the forest. Genaro assumed that all had met their fate suddenly and without a clue.

He then checked the tree line ahead. All looked normal, but upon more scrutiny, Genaro saw a spattering of smaller trees mixed in among the others of the forest. Their trunks seemed oddly thin but were heavily leaved as all the other trees. Some even had vines that seemed to crawl up upon them. And so, Genaro initially dismissed these strange trees as nothing more than a different kind of forest growth.

"Anything to report?" quipped Mr. Clifton, getting a little impatient.

"No sir," replied Genaro, uncertainty in his voice. He had a funny feeling. "But just to be sure, let's cross this field one at a time, with plenty of space between us."

"Better yet, Maple and I will scout ahead while the rest of you wait here," the officer said. "Then we can all join up on the far side."

"Be careful, sir," said Genaro.

"We will," replied Mr. Clifton. "Maple, take your pistol out and stand ready."

As the two men started across the field, Genaro went back to his scanning, focusing his sharp eyes on the far tree line once again.

There was no change in the situation as Mr. Clifton, followed by Maple, crossed the field. As they came upon the first body, the officer briefly squatted down for a closer look, then got up and resumed walking toward the jungle's edge, now only fifteen yards further. Maple followed, ten yards back.

It was just then that Genaro picked up a motion among the skinny trees, a movement where none should have been. A movement that revealed the terrible truth. On one of the trees nearest the clearing, a limb started to rise up, its end moving to point to Mr. Clifton. And for Genaro, as an optical illusion suddenly revealed itself, the scene before him changed!

He was not looking at trees.

These things were tall natives! Tall…how can that be?

These natives, and now he saw many of them, were somehow high up in the canopy. There! He could see that their feet and legs were lashed to tall poles, which, a short time ago, he thought were tree trunks. A flashback from the time he saw a circus performance when he was a child gave him the answer…stilts! The natives were on camouflaged stilts! And one of them was raising something to his mouth. A Blowgun!

"Stop, Clifton. Stop!" Genaro yelled out as loudly as he could, all sense of protocol gone. He had to get them out of danger! He saw both men halt their walking and turn toward him.

But it was too late. The first native fired his blowgun. If it made a sound, Genaro did not hear it. But he and the others did see the officer clasp a hand onto his neck, then his body stiffened, and he fell. Maple saw it, too. His reaction was to immediately start running back, a move that, no doubt, saved his life. Genaro assumed that Maple's swift move brought him out of range of the blowguns, and nothing else was fired at him as he continued his run across the field. But Genaro did notice some stirring among the natives. It was an easy decision for him, therefore, to order everyone back to the ship.

"What about Mr. Clifton?" asked Samuelson rather harshly. "We can't just leave him."

"I want to go back too," replied Genaro, "but it would mean the death of us all. Mr. Clifton is as dead as the others; we all saw him fall. Now, let's get out of here."

With that, they all made their way back to the beach. They then pushed the boat off the sand and rowed back to the Marybelle. Though there were no signs of attack by the natives, each man felt lucky to be alive.

After reporting the incident to the captain, Genaro was told that the other boat had indeed found a supply of water and an abundance of papayas. The captain then weighed anchor and brought the Marybelle closer to the freshwater stream. Yet another expedition was then sent ashore, and a large quantity of the emergency supplies was secured, thankfully, without incident. Shortly thereafter, the Marybelle set sail to continue her original assignment.

After a few days at sea, when the mumbling had died down a bit, and the crew had resumed their normal at-sea routine, the captain assembled everyone, brought them all up to date, and conducted a memorial ceremony for those who had been lost. All understood the risks involved and the decision not to attempt to recover the bodies. The heroic actions by Kacy and Mr. Clifton were acknowledged. Genaro was also given an honorable mention. And so, the incident came to a close.

The tale was told for many years in harbor towns throughout the land, but like most, it eventually faded from knowledge. But in seaside marinas all over, to this day, it is not uncommon to come across a small boat or other run-about bearing the name "Clifton," "Kacy," or "Genaro," even if no one remembers why.

Interview: Fireman

"Good morning, everyone! This is Arty Watson at WKNY in Buntner, New Jersey. Today, I will be interviewing two of Buntner's bravest: fireman Frank Connelly, a twenty-eight-year veteran, and Bobby Hulslander, who has been on the force now for five years. Good morning, gentlemen."

FRANK: Good morning.

BOBBY: Good morning. It is good to be here.

ARTY: Okay, then. I guess the first question is the obvious one… what is it like to be a fireman? What is the job really like? I mean, everyone sees and hears you guys as you race to an emergency, but after we pull back onto the road or after you pass out of earshot, we go back to our regular lives. What do you say, Frank?

FRANK: Well, that is certainly true, unless, of course, you are the one that needs saving, or it is your house on fire. The truth is, we are constantly on standby, ready to go. Sure, our primary job is to extinguish fires and conduct rescues, but that includes a lot of things on many different levels. Every job is different. If I could sum up what we do in one phrase, it would be *"a little bit of everything."*

ARTY: Interesting. What do you think, Bobby?

BOBBY: Frank is right. I haven't been on the job nearly as long as he has, but in my time so far, I've been called upon to help the elderly up and down stairs, pump water out of basements, all the way up to hosing down a giant warehouse fire. The variety of calls is endless, and we are expected to handle it all.

ARTY: What about between jobs, you know, the time when you are not responding? What do you do then?

FRANK: Good question. A lot of people think we hang around all day or night just watching television or sleeping away from home. In reality, there is much to do at the firehouse.

ARTY: Like what?

FRANK: First off, our equipment has to always be maintained. Everything from the fire engines themselves to the hoses, tools, and even our boots and gloves have to be checked, cleaned and checked again to make sure they are ready to go at all times. You don't want to discover a split firehouse when you are using it.

BOBBY: People need to realize that our lives depend on our equipment. It has to work perfectly every time we use it. Our air bottles need to be filled or replaced after each use, the gauges and air hoses checked constantly, and things like that.

FRANK: And the other major thing is the training. We are constantly evolving, not only with equipment but methods, too. Bobbby mentioned the breathing equipment, for example. The air packs that we use have improved greatly over the years. We now have a Heads-Up Display that gives us critical information right on our facemasks. Every time something like this comes up, it comes with the training requirement as well.

ARTY: Well, there has to be some downtime. Especially here in Buntner. We live in a small, quiet town, don't we?

BOBBY: Of course. This is not a major city, and we don't get as many calls as some of the areas' larger departments, but believe me, we are kept busy.

ARTY: Some townspeople think that Buntner should go with a completely volunteer fire department to save money. What about that?

FRANK: Not a good idea, Arty. One of the key elements to a successful rescue, and certainly, a fire, is the quick response. I have known some really good volunteer departments over the years, but you just can't replace a twenty-four-hour fire department when it comes to response time. And on many occasions, that can be the difference between life and death or a merely damaged structure to one that is a complete loss.

ARTY: What do you say, Bobby?

BOBBY: Well, Frank certainly hit on the main point, reaction time. But there is also the issue of a community's peace of mind. Our town's residents know that if there is an emergency, any emergency at all, they are covered, not only by police protection but by a professional fire department and ambulance crew. And that protection is for everyone, not just select groups. Many people have told me that they feel a lot safer as things are around here than if we were all volunteers. They see it as their taxes well spent. Cut the budget somewhere else, not with the fire department.

ARTY: Okay. Next up. What about war stories? Frank, could you tell us about one of your calls that stands out among all the others? In all your time in the fire department, you must have had a few real big events, something that stands out in your memory.

FRANK: Yeah, Sure… there were many huge events during my time so far. Like the time that train full of chemicals derailed outside of town or when Abbott's Used Cars was set on fire, the entire lot of cars went up. There were a few other big fires that I was involved in and many rescues, too, but the one I will always remember was way back in my earliest days.

I was only about two years on the job when we got a frantic call from a woman that her neighbor's house was on fire. She knew the husband was away, and the wife was alone with her two young children.

When we got there, the mother was already outside holding a baby, but she was frantic. Her other child was still inside, and a few of her neighbors were moving toward the house. The house was, by now, fully involved, flames everywhere.

I got my air pack on, checked the gauges, and went up to the mother. She told me the boy's room was on the second floor, up the stairs and on the left. I knew I couldn't wait for the water, so I ran into the burning house.

The stairs were just starting to burn, so I knew I had little time to get the kid. As I ran up the stairs, I yelled, *"Where are you?"* several times. It was only when I got up to the second floor that I heard someone coughing. By this time, the flames were chasing me, and part of me heard the hissing as the water, finally being put into play, hit the fire on the walls of the second floor. I crashed through the door to the back bedroom and once again heard a cough. It was coming from under the bed. I lifted the bed up, and there he was, a little boy no more than six. He looked really scared, but there was no time for words. I scooped him up, pulled him into my chest, and covered him with my arm as best I could. I turned and ran through the flames. It was only a few quick steps down the hall and then down the stairs, but it seemed like forever. I remember praying that the stairs wouldn't collapse while I was on them, and just as I really began to feel the heat, it was over, and I was outside. I saw the mother but ran past her because I saw the ambulance had pulled up. I knew the kid needed some medical attention, so I ran up to Dietrich, one of our EMTs at the time, and handed the kid over to him. I remember the medics going over me, but I got away with it without a scratch. The boy suffered only minor smoke inhalation trauma but ended up just fine.

I was the local hero for a while before all that nonsense died down, but for me, the best part was that it was my first real rescue., and it reinforced my commitment to the job. I knew then what my calling was, and I have felt that way ever since.

ARTY: Wow! That's' quite a story.

BOBBY: That was you?

FRANK: What do you mean?

BOBBY: That was you who pulled that little boy out of the house?

FRANK: Yeah. Why?

BOBBY: That story you just told about the rescue. Well…I saw it much differently.

FRANK: What are you talking about?

BOBBY: Let me tell it this way.

When I was little, I used to get nightmares, I guess like most little kids. But rather than think the bogeyman was under the bed, I thought hiding under the bed would be safe for me. The bogeyman would not find me there. So, every time I had a nightmare, I would get up and go under the bed and go back to sleep. My mom would find me there in the morning once in a while back then.

One night, I woke up while I was under the bed. I was coughing, and as I awoke, I saw the air was thick with smoke. It smelled like fireplace smoke. It scared me a little, but I thought I would be safe under the bed. Then, I heard loud noises that scared me even more. A giant was stomping up the stairs, yelling for me. *"Where are you?"* I heard. It was very scary. Then, I heard the giant coming down the hallway toward my room. Suddenly, my door was slammed open, and there he was! There was a huge, dark giant filling the doorway, a big shadow with a shiny face. The scariest part was that behind him and all around was smoke and fire, gigantic flames from floor to ceiling. It was terrifying, and I started to cry even as I was coughing. This was worse than any of my nightmares.

Then, this giant reached under my bed and, with one hand, lifted the whole thing up in the air. Before I could crawl away, he reached out with his other hand and snatched me up like I weighed nothing at all. He lifted me up to his face and let go of the bed. As it crashed to the floor, the giant pulled me close to his chest and turned into the fire. He ran with me across the hall and down the stairs through the flames.

Then suddenly, we were outside. My eyes hurt, but I could see my mother running to me with Jimmy in her arms. But the giant ignored her and ran me over to the ambulance. Another grownup then took me from the giant and put a mask on my face as I fell asleep again.

I was that kid, Frank. Amazing. I was that kid you rescued that day!

ARTY: Well…how about that, folks.

FRANK: That was you? I don't believe it.

BOBBY: Believe it, Frank. It was me. I spent two days in the hospital but recovered completely. The house was destroyed, but between the insurance and some help from our neighbors, my parents bought another house in town less than six months later.

As I grew older, I felt the calling too. Since then, I have always wanted to be a fireman. I was a fireman in the Navy, and as soon as I came home, I took the test for Buntner.

ARTY: And you never knew it was Frank who saved you?

BOBBY: No…no. Not until just now.

ARTY: Well, this has been an amazing turn of events, much more than I expected today. I want to thank both Bobby and Frank for coming in and sharing with us some facts about their profession and that fantastic coincidence of a story. Until next week, this is Arty Watson of KNY, Buntner, signing off.

Blown Away

It was Anderson's first major deployment as a sailor on his ship. He was fresh out of his rating school, fresh off leave with his family, and only two weeks aboard. His ship was the USS Barnstable County, a modern-era amphibious tank landing ship. They had gotten underway on May tenth and picked up a contingent of marines at Camp Lejeune the next morning. And now they were at sea, mostly across *"the pond,"* Navy slang for the Atlantic Ocean, and approaching their first European port. It was to be a six-month cruise, and a first stop to Rota, Spain, was in order for the transfer to the Mediterranean fleet.

All went well until a day and a half out of Rota, a storm hit. A storm that popped out of nowhere. A storm that hit the Barnstable County so quickly that there was no time to turn away from it for a safer course. Anderson had been warned that any storm at sea could be a real threat to the ship. He had been trained in the basics of moving about the ship, working, and even eating on the mess deck in rough seas but had only experienced a few samples of mild rocking and rolling up to this point.

And now this.

Word came down to *"secure ship for heavy seas."* And so, the crew inspected all the spaces, securing any loose tools, machinery, and

equipment. Special *"bag meals"* were prepared for the crew and the marines by the cooks. The marines themselves were kept busy ensuring that the heavy cables that held the vehicles and gear to the main deck and the tank deck below were tightened to full capacity. All seemed ready for the approaching storm.

As it happened, the ship took the storm head-on, with the waves coming at the ship one after another directly toward the bow. Things weren't too bad at first, and it gave everyone time to recheck items that turned out not to be completely secure.

Then things got much worse. The bow of the ship started impacting larger and larger waves. *"Green water over the bow"* was heard over the 1MC several times as Barnstable County slammed into the wind-driven sea. Metallic creaks and groans were heard throughout the ship as the structure itself flexed to accommodate the strain. Soon after, all non-essential crew and all marines were ordered into their racks for safety, just to ride things out. All work was canceled. The mess deck was closed to all hands. Even the bag meals were only given to those on watch. Survival became the mission.

This went on for hours. Anderson was blown away by his personal feelings of panic and despair. The only thing that kept him from losing it completely was the fact that his shipmates seemed to be taking it all in stride. They had been through this before, and to them, it was just another part of Navy life. But for Anderson, a first-timer, it was terrifying. Each time the ship dropped off a wave crest and crashed into the forward roll of the next one, the shudder was felt along the entire ship. Anderson had to hang onto both bunk rails just to avoid being flung up to the steel overhead above. Sleep was impossible, and there was not even a sense of rest.

Finally, Barnstable County passed out of the worst of the storm. The slamming became less intense, and there was a sense that all was returning to normal. After a while, *"Continue ship's work"* was passed, and everyone reported to their workstations to assess and repair any damage.

Anderson was tasked with assisting the other Hull Technicians to check the water levels in the ballast tanks to ensure that no unexpected flooding had occurred. The HTs also had to reweld a couple of the main deck railings that had been snapped by the raging sea.

Anderson later found out that one sailor had *"fallen up a ladder"* below deck during the storm. Hobbes had the deck suddenly drop out from under him just as he was taking a step up a set of stairs. Because he did not have both hands on the railings, the sudden movement caused him to fly upward and hit his head on the overhead, and he was knocked out. Fortunately, others around him saw what had happened and brought Hobbes down to sick bay. There, he regained consciousness, was placed under observation, and was finally released a few days later. Two other sailors suffered minor ankle injuries, and one marine ended up with a broken arm, but overall, no serious injuries or loss of equipment occurred. Things could have been much worse.

The only good thing that came out of the storm for Anderson was that he was congratulated for surviving his first encounter with an angry sea. The waves had been up to forty feet high, and the winds had been at gale force. His conduct during the storm had been closely watched by his shipmates, and he *"passed the test."* His journey from being a new guy to being an experienced one had begun.

The Competition

It was a simple contest, a straightforward competition. The winner would live to be set free, and the loser would die. All Roger had to do was beat his opponent to the plateau on the mountain before him, only five miles away. He had slept well, eaten well, and felt in great shape as the time to begin approached. He and another Special Operations soldier had been captured by an enemy who seemed to have a sense of humor.

The other, Roger's competition, was unknown to him and would indeed be starting the same quest from another location. The plan was that they would never meet except at the end, when the first to arrive had to kill the other when he, too, reached the plateau. Roger had been told that his opponent was from the other side, and since they were sworn enemies, he knew he would be able to kill him. A weapon would be awaiting the winner at the plateau.

"Are you ready, dog?" Roger nodded his head, and soon after, his blindfold was removed. He had but a few moments to orient himself toward the mountain before the command, *"Then, go!"* was shouted near his ear. With not even a look back, Roger started running across the scrub desert. He half expected to be shot as he started his quest, but nothing happened. After running a few hundred yards, Roger afforded

himself a brief look back at his captors, but they had already loaded up, and their vehicle had started away.

Roger then refocused his attention on the job at hand. He could only assume his opponent had been given the same sort of send-off and was now racing toward the plateau as well. *"No time to waste,"* thought Roger as he picked up the pace.

The scrub desert had a series of threats that Roger had to avoid as he ran on. He knew all about the unevenness of the terrain, the threat of stepping in holes in the ground or slipping on loose rocks, let alone the sharp thorns and needles of the unfriendly plant life. The lack of shade in the hot late morning sun did not help either, but Roger had survived much worse.

Soon enough, the scrub desert gave way to a series of gentle slopes that began in the foothills of the mountain. Here, the surface changed to a thicker soil type and a mix of low bushes and small trees. The atmosphere seemed a little cooler here as shade from the trees became more and more frequent. As he ran up the increasing slope of the hillside, Roger began to feel the first suggestion of fatigue throughout his body but pushed on, knowing his quest was not only to reach the plateau but to get there first.

At one point, Roger heard the sound of running water ahead, and just after the terrain had somewhat leveled off. A few more running steps brought him to a small but powerful stream of mountain water. No sooner had he broken through to the stream than Roger got a big surprise. A leopard squatted before him, not ten feet away, belly close to the ground, busily lapping up water from a small pool off the stream.

As he skidded to a stop, Roger's hand went instinctively to the sheath knife on his right hip. As he realized in horror that his knife was not there, the leopard took notice of Roger's presence. Both reacted the same way. As Roger leaped back away from the cat, the leopard did the same, but rather than just freeze as Roger had done, the cat ran away at nearly lightning speed. Roger watched it depart as the rush of adrenaline caused him to tense up for a fight that, thank goodness, did not occur. He stood in silent amazement for several seconds, had his moment of relief, and shook his head as he started to cross the stream. Midway, Roger allowed himself a few seconds of immersion to cool himself off both physically and emotionally. He had dodged quite a bullet with the leopard encounter but had to get back to his quest. After taking a few swallows of the water, Roger left the stream and resumed his journey uphill.

Here, the woods started to thicken. The trees became larger, and more of the sunlight was blocked. As a result, things seemed much quieter, and Roger began to hear his own breathing as he now alternated from a run to a fast walk. For the first time, he thought of his opponent. *"Surely, he must be going through the same struggles I am experiencing."* Such thoughts, Roger knew, were both comforting and dangerous as they took his mind off his quest. *"No more drifting off."* Roger chastised himself as he, again, quickened his pace.

Finally, after what had to have been a mile or two, the terrain once again changed. This time, from less wood to more rocks. Roger knew he was approaching the mountain heights and that the plateau could not be much further. By now, his fatigue was undeniable, but Roger knew how to handle such a condition and yet still maintain the ability to carry on, fight, and prevail. The change to loose rocks and shifting soil forced a bit of a slowdown, but Roger kept pressing forward. His eyes alternated from looking down at his foot placement to up to the pathway ahead.

After some time at this, Roger finally saw the plateau not far ahead. It was shrouded in a group of rock outcroppings but was unmistakable as a large and flat piece of ground. As a matter of routine, Roger started a quick scan for signs of his enemy but saw nothing. And so, he continued on, in a straight line to his objective. As he drew closer, Roger could see different portions of the plateau but not the entire thing. He was certain that he had beaten his opponent to this spot and hurried to complete the trip and find the weapon.

There was one more outcropping of rock that stood in his way. By this time, Roger could see nearly the entire plateau but, as yet, could not find the weapon, some sort of gun he imagined. *"It must be right around this outcropping,"* thought Roger as he pushed forward in a burst of speed to hurry the resolution.

He stepped around the last enormous rock that defined part of the boundary of the plateau. By now, Roger was confident that he had won the race. In moments, he expected to see the gun and have enough time to pick it up and await the arrival of his enemy. *"I won, I won!"* Roger said out loud as he could not help himself from a bit of joy.

"No, you lost," was the last thing Roger heard.

Right Off the Bat

It was our first trip to Virginia Beach for a week-long vacation. We had been driving since the wee hours and finally arrived at a location just north of the resort town. Here, we decided to stop at one of the public areas to get some beach time before checking in to our hotel. It was nearly midday, and the weather was already hot but pleasant. We pulled into one of the parking lots and took a look around.

Right off the bat, we noticed a spot on the beach. It sat at a slightly higher elevation than the rest of the area. Though the beach was crowded with people, this tract was still available, and it seemed we were in luck. So, I quickly found a parking spot, and we started packing out our gear.

"I wonder why no one has claimed that spot," I said as we hurried to get our beach gear out of the van.

"I don't know," Phil replied as he removed the two sand chairs and closed the sliding doors, "but let's grab it before someone else does."

Gloria and Jeannie carried the blanket, towels, and umbrella while Phil and I took the chairs and the cooler. We took the short hike from the parking lot and, after a few minutes, were at the spot. A few tufts of reed grass stuck out, and a few small holes in the sand were here and there, but it all looked peaceful and quite inviting. The immediate area was not overcrowded, but there were many beachgoers scattered around the beach.

As we set up, I noticed more than once some of the other people looking at us, talking about us, and even heard a few laughs.

"What is that all about?" Jeannie had seen the others as well.

"Aah! They are probably just locals making fun of us tourists, that's all." I answered. Since no one approached us with a greeting or anything, we ignored them as we completed laying out the blanket, the cooler, and the sand chairs. We arranged the umbrella so it provided partial shade, more on the chairs than the blanket. The heat of the sun and the warm sea breeze were quite satisfying, and so we decided to go for a swim.

The water was very nice, warm, and comforting, with only small to medium waves. We splashed around for a while, and Phil and I spent some time body surfing when a bigger-than-average set of waves came in. At one point, we encountered dolphins in the water. They would swim very close to shore on occasion and one time came as near as five feet to Jeannie. No one else in the water seemed alarmed by this, so there was no need for us to get excited about it. Actually, the dolphin encounter was amazing.

Sometime later, I had a moment with a stingray. I had been swimming underwater for a while, careful to avoid the occasional other person in the shoulder-deep water. After a while pushing to my limit, I came up for air. I cleared my eyes, looked around, and noticed two things I thought were strange.

First, I was alone in the water. There was no one swimming or standing nearby. Everyone was out of the water except me. Then, I realized something more alarming. Most of the people on the beach, including my friends, were pointing at me. I even heard Gloria shout, *"Look out, Ted!"* Suddenly, I got very nervous and quickly looked around. Was I about to get eaten by a giant shark?

As I turned to look behind me, I saw a stingray floating in the water only three feet away. It was about two feet wide and almost as long with a long, slender tail. It did not seem threatening since it was just floating in the water, but the stinger along its tail was very prominent. I was immediately relieved at not being attacked, but soon after, my curiosity took over. I did not know if this thing was dead or alive since it did not display any independent movement. However, I did know that most aquatic animals cannot swim backward. And so, I slowly approached the stingray. I was very careful not to go near the stinger but reached out and grabbed the very tip of its tail. I then tugged the thing backward. Almost immediately, I felt a surge of resistance as the stingray started to swim forward and away from my pull. It was very much alive. And that was enough for me. I released the tail, swam, and ran to the beach as quickly as I could. Once on the beach, I found my friends.

"Why did you leave me out there?" I was surprised and a little annoyed at having been abandoned like that.

"We yelled for you, but we could not find you," Jeannie said. "We thought you were out of the water already. Where were you?"

"I took a long swim underwater," I responded. "I wanted to see how long I could hold my breath."

"Yeah, and then we saw you come up right in front of the stingray," added Phil. "We were certain you were going to get stung."

"Well, it turned out alright, I guess. Anyway, I have had enough of the ocean for now." They all agreed, and we headed back to our spot to get some sun, the adventure for the day over. Or so we thought.

Once back at our site, we each dried off, took a drink from the cooler, and settled down for a rest. Phil and I adjusted the umbrella to let the full sun fall on the girls as they wanted to work on their tans. Phil and I were less concerned with that and hung out under the umbrella. The combination of the warm breeze and the hot temperature was very soothing. It was surprising at first as we all realized how tired we had become. All was peaceful.

Unfortunately, it was not to last.

It was Gloria who first noticed. "Hey guys, I thought I felt something moving under the blanket." She and Jeannie had stretched out face down on the blanket and had just been dozing off.

"What do you mean, moved? You probably just shifted the sand yourself." Phil was quick with an explanation.

"Okay, okay. No, wait. There it is again. Same spot." Gloria sounded a lot more concerned this time.

Suddenly, Jeannie screamed and sprung up to her feet. "There is something under the blanket. I just felt it, too." Now, both girls were standing, looks of fright on their faces. Phil and I had to act.

"Get off the blanket," I said as Phil reached for the nearest edge. The girls quickly jumped off. Out of the corner of my eye, I noticed several others on the beach now standing up and looking at us.

Phil yanked the blanket up and away with a snapping pull of his arm. And there before us was a disturbing sight. All along the sandy expanse were crabs, small white, nearly transparent crabs coming out of the holes we had earlier noticed but dismissed as a problem. Others were appearing all around us, covering the little hill we had set up on. We all started doing a little dance and running maneuver to avoid getting our feet bitten by these little creatures as we heard a chorus of laughter coming from the others on the beach. We finally reached an area beyond the consortium of crabs, no longer relaxed or tired. We all then realized the scam we had fallen for. Of course, the locals had known about the crab colony. And, of course, they had waited and watched as we set ourselves up for the onslaught. We must have provided them with quite the entertainment.

And the ordeal was not even finished yet. We still had to recover our gear and get the hell out of there. As it turned out, though we knew the tiny crabs were essentially harmless, Phil and I took turns bunny-stepping back out onto the hill and, after a few trips, managed to gather up our chairs, the umbrella, and everything else, before a crowd of many cheering onlookers. Phil and I both had a somewhat moment of satisfaction as we both flashed the finger at our hosts as we departed. Someone hooted, *"You all come back again soon, now!"*

It was not the most welcoming start to our vacation.

The Man at the Door

It all started when someone knocked on Pete's door as he sat in the living room one evening. Upon opening the door, Pete was surprised when this guy, not much bigger than him, pushed past Pete.

He looked around, pulled a gun from his waistband, and said, "Is there anyone else here?" Peter knew he would have to move quickly if he had a chance of getting out of this, so he said, "There is someone in the next room," as Pete nodded toward the kitchen. He knew the guy would look over there, and when he did, Peter attacked.

The man had the gun, a nasty-looking pistol, in his right hand, about waist level, pointing at Peter. He was only three feet in front of him, and Pete thought he had a chance. So, Pete jumped forward with his left foot in the lead, chopped down with his left hand onto the gun-hand as he pivoted to the left. The man was able to get one silent shot off, revealing a murderous intention, before Peter's hand clasped onto his right hand, still holding the pistol.

In the meantime, Pete swung his right arm up, noticing oddly what seemed to be wires, and delivered a palm-down knife blow to the neck, catching the man just under the chin with the inside edge of his right index finger. As the man's attention left the gun, Peter swung his right arm up and past his face, taking him down to the floor and twisting the man's right wrist outward at the same time. His grip on the gun, now loosened, allowed Peter to take the gun from him as he fell, gasping for breath.

Peter briefly thought about all the martial arts training he had taken many years ago as he pointed the strange-looking gun at this guy so he would know all was over when he finally looked back to Pete, but that didn't happen. The man was clearly in dire straits, both hands clasping at his throat, eyes wide in panic, and still struggling just to breathe. Pete went from fighting to first aid. He tossed the gun behind him, dropped down, and tried to help this guy, now just a person trying to stay alive.

Peter loosened the man's shirt and tilted his head back to hopefully open the airway. But the man's hands started flailing in a less and less purposeful way, and his eyes seemed to bulge even larger. Finally, and within only a few seconds, he gave a whole-body lurch and then relaxed as he died. It was very unpleasant for Pete to witness. At that point, he blacked out.

Sometime later, Peter was in his favorite recliner, television off, just reading a book of Sherlock Holmes cases, when he heard a knock on the door. Since he was comfortable just sitting there and not expecting any company, Peter decided to ignore the knocking. He hoped whoever it was would just go away. The knocking, however, persisted. But Pete was determined and refused to answer, ignoring the noise. The man at the door tried yelling something like "…so I can open the door." a few times, but finally, after getting no response, he left, leaving Pete to the welcomed silence he relished.

A few minutes later, Peter heard a low hissing noise that seemed to be coming from the ceiling. There was no sign of a vapor or anything, but the hissing did suggest something being introduced to his living room from an outside source. Curious now, Peter went to stand up to look around to find out what was going on. But as he started to rise, Pete suddenly felt dizzy and somehow could not find the strength in his legs to push him to stand. As he half sat, half fell back into his chair, Pete, with groggy eyes, saw a man at the door, now opened, moving toward him with a gas mask on his head. Then, all faded away.

On another occasion, Peter was doing his workout in the living room when, once again, there was a sound at the front door, more of a commotion on the other side rather than a knock. Suddenly, his door was slammed open, and no less than three or four men rushed him. Peter was pushed off balance, pressed against the wall, and overcome by sheer mass before he could do anything to defend himself. He was also hit in the face by an acrid-smelling spray of some kind, which caused him to scream in agony. Pete was then roughly turned over and felt himself being tied up when, once again, he blacked out.

"Now, this last case presents the most dangerous personality type I have ever seen. This person, ah…Peter Stevenson is a complete schizophrenic. He is very capable as a fighter due to his background in martial arts from when he was a kid. He can and will kill if attacked. He has done so even in this institution. When his attorney went to visit him, not only did Peter not recognize him, but he also saw him as a threat and lunged toward him. The lawyer made a foolish mistake. He knew of his client's condition and thought if things got rough, he would be able to subdue him with a stun gun. It was a fatal miscalculation. When Peter saw the stun gun, he attacked his attorney with such fury that he killed him in less than five seconds. But what shows the true depth of his illness is what he did just after the attack. The lawyer had his windpipe crushed and didn't die instantly but rather spent his final moments struggling to breathe. And when Pete saw this, his instinct then became to try to save the man's life. Of course, he couldn't do anything to help, and when the lawyer finally died, Peter's emotional reaction was so severe, it caused him to pass out."

Dr. Philmore was addressing his fellow psychiatrists at one of their societies' many conferences. The overall discussions focused on the treatments provided to the most dangerous of the criminally insane patients in their care.

"The patient had no recollection of this event despite all attempts to prompt him to relive it. Hypnosis, drugs, nothing worked, and he was returned to his cell shortly afterward. He was normally quiet and content with his situation, and many of us believe he was living in his own fantasy world. And that was okay, except for the times when attempts were made to bring him out of his cell for testing and treatment.

"On one such occasion, he ignored all attempts to get him to move to the back of his cell so the guards could enter to prepare him for transport to the infirmary. We finally had to use an aerosol sleep agent to subdue him. And once again, when all was over, Pete did not remember a thing. But using aerosols in such a manner has since been classified as inhumane, and we no longer use them.

"And so, it was finally decided to leave Pete alone. He seemed to have no self-awareness of his condition and literally lived only in the moment. His physical abilities cannot be erased, and so he is considered a deadly threat in every encounter. So, for the most part, we left him alone. He has a television in his cell and a variety of books to read but, of course, no electronics of any kind. His medications were given to him and mixed into his food and drink, and he was never allowed visitors. Whenever he needed to be removed from his cell for any reason, well, the guards had to go in as a Cell Extraction Team. From Pete's perspective, it was always a home invasion. No amount of negotiation seemed to help him understand the truth. Part of his mind just shut down. He passed out, then woke up again to face a new reality, with no recollection at all."

"What is an example of this *New Reality Syndrome*, Doctor Philmore?" asked one of his colleagues.

"Well, whenever he was removed from his cell, we were careful not to expose him to any other patient during his transfer to the infirmary. Even there, he was kept in isolation except for the doctors and technicians, all male, by the way, who were attending him. A fully uniformed and outfitted guard was also always present, with at least two others just outside the door. He was always restrained, either in his chair or otherwise, for his own safety and everyone else's too. It was a situation that should have been obvious to anyone. But Pete never saw it that way. When he looked around at the situation he was in, he saw it much differently. To him, he was a regular person with no understanding of why he was being treated as he was. He claimed to have no memories of his past behaviors and seemed willing to cooperate in any way *'to get this over with so I can go home.'* Attempts to explain the real situation to him resulted in both emphatic denials and, in most cases, agitation and outbursts, resulting in the guards needing to step in."

"And what now, since his escape?" asked another of the doctors.

"Well, as you know, I am part of the extensive multi-unit task force now looking for him. I cannot emphasize the significance of finding Peter Stevenson and returning him to custody. His level of threat to the public is off the charts. He shows no hesitation to escalate from utter calmness to complete and merciless violence with no sense of remorse or concern for his own safety. His method of escape proves that."

"And just how did he manage to get out of here, doctor? This looks very high security to me," observed a third colleague.

"We don't know all the details even now," responded Doctor Philmore. "We know that the guard broke several rules by going into Pete's cell alone and without notifying anyone else. But how he was lured in there, we will probably never know. There was evidence that the guard was tortured, probably to give up his codes, then his clothes were swapped with Stevenson's, and we think Pete just walked out with the shift change. It could have been as easy as that."

"As far as what's next, that is really up to the FBI, who has the lead on the task force. I am just a consultant at this point. I told them that Stevenson knew he was being hunted. But I do know one thing. When they do find Pete and move in to get him–I would not want to be the man at the door."

Proceed and Persist

I was in my martial arts school, on the mat, and taking a test called Line-up Kumite. It was one of the tests I needed to pass to acquire my first-degree brown belt, one level shy of the black belt.

And so, I had quite a few skills going into this situation. This was a fighting test as well as one of endurance. I had to fight against a line of my fellow students, only one at a time, for sixty seconds, but one after another in a steady stream. The line of opponents was comprised of six others, all of differing ranks and experience levels, the lowest being only two ranks below mine. Each came at me fresh and at maximum speed with the full intention of scoring points against me. The endurance challenge came in with the fact that I had to go through the line three times and only allow a limited number of points to be scored against me.

The main challenge to this test, however, was how I would balance things out. With opponents at my skill level or even above it, I was forced to perform at my highest levels, and both score some points and not get scored on. With those of lesser skills, there was an opportunity to relax and even rest a little as the sparring took place. But the added challenge was that Sensei, the head instructor, was the one who selected which of my opponents was next and the order of those in the line I was to fight. It was yet another variable I could not control.

In our school, there was extensive training in what is called *"controlled contact."* Kicks and punches to the body were delivered with enough force to let both parties know when an attack scored a point but not enough to actually crack a rib or cause any other serious damage. Contact of any kind to the face or groin was never allowed and was judged as a score against the person making the contact during a test. The idea was that we, as a school, could not sanction harm to our students. We all had to go to school or work the next day, after all.

As I went through the line the first time, I was surprised at how well I did. Three of the six were at my skill level, one much better and faster, and only two that presented less of a challenge. Nick, the Sensei, saved the best for last, but even after that flurry of high-intensity sparring, I had only been scored on once. I was pleased with my performance so far, and as I took my ten-second rest between the lines, I felt confident I would pass the test.

After the second round, I was not so sure. During this line-up, I had let my guard down too much against one of the easy opponents, and he scored on me not once but twice. Surprised and embarrassed, I knew I would have to redouble my efforts to proceed and persist to win the day. But, by this time, the endurance element of the test was starting to become more of a factor. Whereas my opponents only fought me once in six turns, I was getting no rest between them. And when they first came out against me, each opponent came with all they had.

The combat took on a life of its own. I had entered a realm where there was no conscious thought, no time for planning, considering options, or trying new things. The focus was one hundred percent on the here and now, the drive to attack an opening and defend against incoming. Time seemed to be taken out of the equation. There was no audience, no mat, no place, only my opponent and me. We had all been trained to look not at the eyes but the chest of our opponent so as not to be distracted by facial expressions but only react to movements by the body's core. The only cue I responded to was the word *"Next"* when my opponent would back off, only to be replaced by another charging enemy.

Finally, my mind heard *"Break,"* and I was granted that, by now, a somewhat confusing interval of time between line-up two and the dreaded third round. By now, I was breathing hard and fully aware of it. I did my best to control my breathing as I had been taught to do, but I knew I had to remain at my highest performance level possible because…. here it comes.

"Next" registered in my ears as John, my toughest opponent of them all, charged at me with a smile on his face. My eyes snapped off his face and to his chest as I quickly parried a straight punch he threw to my head. We fought at a frantic pace, and I almost welcomed the feel of all-out combat again. When we were done, I had scored twice on him, but John had gotten a good shot on me as well.

"Next," "next," and "next" were heard only through a haze as the seemingly endless third round continued. The one thing I do remember of that time was when I messed up and hit an adversary in the face with a little too much contact. He shook it off and continued, but it had been a serious error on my part, a slippage of judgment because my fatigue level was near its limit.

Finally, the test was over. Nick said, *"Rest,"* and everyone stopped. As tired as I was, I knew that if I had to go on, I probably could have. I really would not feel tired until the adrenaline wore off. We all performed to the Sensei first, then to each other, a series of quick bows that denoted the respect we all had for each other. And with that, my test came to a close.

All eyes turned to Nick as he made his judgment. I knew I had been scored at least four times and did not know what the limit was. But all my budding doubts were dispelled as Nick approached me with a smile on his face and his right hand extended out.

"Congratulations!" was what he said.

Pheasanting

We had all agreed to meet in the big field after an hour of hunting. There was no problem with that because, by then, most of the stocked birds were taken. We had started in different fields, and most of us had at least one bird in the pouch by then. Eddy and Danny had started in the big field along with Eddy's Brittany, Mandy, so both had gotten a great opportunity at flushing pheasants. Eddy had a day for the record books, and Danny ended up with a huge rooster. Joey and Jimmy had started up in the higher fields along the lower slopes of the mountain.

They had not done as well, with only one pheasant in the pouch for Jimmy. And then there was my son, David, and me. We had tried our luck in the field alongside the big field, just past the stream that coursed between the two of them. David was only thirteen at the time and was just going through his third hunting season with us. Though he was still working his way through the basics, he had made a good crossing shot on a rooster pheasant and did not seem to mind the extra weight in his hunting vest. I had also managed to down a bird, a nice-sized hen.

Pheasant hunting is very popular in New Jersey. Though the birds do not occur naturally in our state, there is an entire industry set up to

ensure thousands of ringneck pheasants are made available throughout the land to be hunted. Pheasants are raised in both state-run and privately owned facilities, nourished and cared for each year to ensure a large population of mature birds are available for the November to February hunting season.

During the season, pheasants are stocked on state Wildlife Management Areas (WMAs) and portions of two National Recreation Areas (NRAs) and purchased for private hunting club properties as well. Though pen-raised, pheasants adapt easily to the woods and fields of New Jersey and present quite a challenge to hunters. The problem is that they are ground nesting birds and, as such, are quite vulnerable to predators such as foxes, owls, eagles, and coyotes, to name a few. This prevents the development of any indigenous population. And so, the birds are stocked on state land three times each week during the season.

In order to hunt pheasants, one must first acquire a hunting license by completing a hunter/safety course. Once that is done, the prospective new hunter must demonstrate a knowledge of gun handling and shooting skills in the field to an instructor. Only after these two requirements are met can one purchase a general license allowing the use of a shotgun for hunting small game and deer. Additionally, a pheasant stamp must be purchased for the upland bird season. All licenses and stamps must be repurchased each year and prominently displayed on the hunter while in the field.

In addition to getting licensed, a hunter needs the proper equipment. This includes specific clothing. The boots must be high enough to provide support and comfort in terrain that can be rocky and steep to swampy and muddy, thick with snow, or slick with ice. Many hunters split the season with several pairs of boots depending on the weather. The guidance is similar with pants and shirts. Since the pheasant hunting season in New Jersey spans days of warm weather to those either rainy, snowy or bitterly cold, one must have a variety of clothing to handle the weather. The adage *"Don't dress for now, dress for five hours from now"* certainly applies.

In all cases, gloves and a blaze orange hat are necessary, and a pheasant jacket or vest must be worn outside of everything else. This garment must have a large area of blaze orange material to help hunters see each other while afield. The jacket or vest must also have a grip for the hunter's license holder as well as specific pockets to hold things like extra shotgun shells, hand warmers, and gloves, as well as a large pouch in the back for any taken birds.

The most important piece of equipment for the pheasant hunter is the shotgun. For the most part, twelve-gauge or twenty-gauge shotguns are used, but some hunters select other gauges as well. The type of shotgun also varies. Some hunters prefer a pump shotgun or a semi-auto shotgun. These guns allow the loading and firing of three shots, the most allowed in a gun while hunting in New Jersey. Others prefer a double-barreled shotgun, either over-under or side-by-side. While these guns only carry two shells, they allow the presence of two different chokes on the same gun, one for each barrel. This feature optimizes the spread of the shot while shooting at the pheasants. This makes up for the loss of a third shot in the eyes of many hunters.

When all is said and done, the most important element for any pheasant hunter is gun handling. For all the talk of guns and shooting, pheasant hunting is a safe sport, as statistics go. This is due to the seriousness most hunters take about the sport. While walking the fields or hills, a hunter is carrying a loaded shotgun. The gun safety must be on, but all hunters are trained not to trust any mechanical safety. True safety is controlling where the barrel is pointing. Special care must be taken so as to not ever point a loaded shotgun at another hunter. There are various ways to carry a shotgun that ensure it is always pointed in a safe direction, and hunters need to know the different carries before they go afield.

Gun handling is especially important when an opportunity comes up. When the pheasant flushes and starts to fly away, the hunter must be fully aware of all that is around him or her. Most of the time, a flushing pheasant is unexpected, and the hunter may be a little shocked by the sudden explosion of the bird as it comes up off the ground. This is the moment of truth. The hunter must shoot safely and only at the pheasant. There is no excuse for putting a fellow hunter in danger for the sake of a pheasant or any other game animal. Taking the shot is secondary to safety, a tenet expected of all hunters.

The pairings for this particular hunt were based on experience. Eddy, Danny, and I were seasoned hunters, and Jimmy and Joey had more than a few seasons behind them as well. David was the novice, and I wanted to be able to help him refine the craft on that morning.

As we walked our field earlier, we noticed others were there as well. I made sure David knew where the others were at all times, and on one occasion, he did not shoot at a flying bird as it would have threatened the other hunters. We ended up losing the pheasant to the other group, but I was glad he made the right decision and told him so. Later on, as we walked toward the end of the field, a rooster pheasant got up just in front of me and flew across David's position. He calmly took his shot, and down it went. Soon after, we were heading toward the stream, this time walking along the perimeter of the field to meet our buddies for the meeting. It was time for another lesson.

"Now, I know that others have passed through this area before, but you still have to be alert. Sometimes, the pheasant hunkers down and doesn't flush when someone walks by. They are very hard to spot when still, but sometimes you can see the white ring around the neck of the male birds and even the eyes. There could be a pheasant anywhere along here."

We were just along the edge of the field, with only about fifteen feet of woods between us and the dirt road, an area in which I did not expect to see any action. So, David's response sounded strange.

"Like that one," he said as he pointed down to the right. And sure enough, there was a hen bird, as nice as you please, just sitting there among the shrubs, staring at us. We quickly set up, and on signal, I stepped in and flushed the pheasant. David had the first shot as I really wanted him to limit out, but he missed, and it was my backup shot that brought the hen-bird down. It ended up quite the tale when, shortly after, we met up with the others.

We all ended up at the prescribed location in the big field at about the same time. Eddy and Danny were planning to leave early and put in some work for the day. The rest of us were eager to continue the hunt. But we all made time for this gathering, a tradition of sorts, to trade stories and just spend some time in conversation.

We stood in the field, near the hedgerow by the road, in a semi-circle. David told our story first and took a few friendly hits for missing his last shot. And I took some heat for not letting David empty his gun at the bird. All in good fun.

Jimmy and Joey ended up having only a single encounter. They were both walking uphill in the woods next to an overgrown field, with Joey about ten feet ahead and to the left of Jimmy. Suddenly, a rooster got up between them and started running uphill away from Jimmy, only a few feet away. When it saw Joey up ahead, the pheasant abruptly turned around, and no sooner did it start running downhill than it took off into the air. Since Jimmy already knew a running pheasant would nearly always choose to fly when going downhill, he got quickly ready and downed the bird with his first shot. Joey said it was the best shot he had ever seen.

As for Eddy and Danny, the hunt was a very quick one. With Mandy running figure eight in front of them, both hunters had a big advantage. The dog gleefully did the work and sought out the pheasants with an eagerness and a nose that could not be measured. Barely forty yards into the field, Mandy flushed up three pheasants that had remained together since being stocked the night before. A rare event, but it does happen on occasion. Danny took the first shot but missed. Then Eddy, with his short-barreled twelve-gauge side-by-side old Italian Bertarelli shotgun, got doubles, that is, two quick shots for two pheasants down. His day was over ten minutes after starting from the road.

As for Danny, well, Mandy wasn't done. Rather than run to the downed pheasants, Mandy ran off to the right, where she had scented yet another pheasant. She flushed it, and Danny, who knew to always trust the dog, got his pheasant for the day, the biggest rooster of them all, as it turned out.

After we had all told our renditions of the morning's events, the conversation shifted to other times and places. My attention level dropped a bit, and I started taking in details of our surroundings. The wind, though never strong on this day, had died down completely, and all was calm. The part of the field we were in was composed of long, green grass, mostly folded over and matted. It provided a very comfortable area to stand on, and we were all quite relaxed.

Except for Mandy.

I had noticed earlier that Mandy was not as calm as would be expected. Rather, Eddy's dog seemed to be restless, constantly moving along. Her behavior seemed out of place. She would walk outside of our circle, then inside, and sometimes in between a couple of us, but never still.

"What's up with Mandy?" I finally asked Ed.

"I don't know, but she does seem a bit birdy, "he replied.

Just then, an extraordinary thing happened. Mandy suddenly charged toward the very center of the circle we had all been standing in. She seemed just to be ready to pounce when there was a stirring in the layered grass right in front of her. And then, from that movement, a pheasant exploded upward. The thing had been hiding in the grass all that time and never flushed as we all arrived to essentially surround it. It probably would have stayed there all day if Mandy had not sniffed it out.

As it happened, the pheasant lifted off with a squawk and a flurry of feathers, with Mandy leaping up just behind it. As one, we all stood there for a second or two, in complete shock as to what happened. Joey, who was on the end, reacted first, brought his gun up, and shot. But he was too quick and missed. David also tried his luck but also missed. My double was broken open, and with no shells in the barrels, I was out of the game. And by the time Jimmy took his two Hail Mary shots, the pheasant was out of range. We started to look at each other in disbelief, and a few of us started to laugh, but the action was not yet over.

I was still looking at the pheasant as it continued to fly across the field. Sometimes, they fly only a short distance and land again. This could give you a second chance at the pheasant, and there were still most of us who had not yet got our limit of two birds for the day. I was pleased to see that the bird appeared to fly lower and get set to land.

Suddenly, a huge bird, which looked like a red-tailed hawk, swooped out of the sky and snatched our pheasant up like it was a sparrow. The rooster had no warning and must have died instantly. The hawk dipped down a little after taking on the weight of the pheasant but, with a few flaps of its enormous wings, quickly recovered and flew off.

We stood there in silence, witnessing the spectacle until the hawk was lost to sight. None of us had ever seen anything like that before. But as fascinating as it had been, the event was a bit humbling, too. Six of us, all hunters with at least some experience, had not been able to take down a pheasant that had literally started flying from our very feet. And just at the end of it, our second chance had been denied by a hawk, of all things, just another hunter looking for a meal.

We split up after that. Eddy and Danny went home. Joey and Jimmy ended up staying for the morning, each finishing with one pheasant. David and I hunted the big field for a while but had no more action and left about an hour later.

But, as the years have gone by, that pheasant hunting trip remains one of our best.

Today's the Day

Today's the day.

Memorial Day was right around the corner, and he had been putting this off for too long now, one excuse after another, but no longer. "I don't care if it takes all day," he thought. *"This is it."*

As Tony woke up, he did his first leg exercises of the day while still lying prone in bed. Just a little leg pumping under the covers to get the juices flowing. The doctor had told him to lubricate the knee joints first before moving about, and Tony knew the value of such advice.

Knee pumps over with, Tony got up and out of bed slowly to minimize the pain. The first test was standing up, but today, the knees seemed alright. Next was the first few steps, usually the toughest part, but again, today, not so bad. The arthritis gave him more of an ache than a stabbing pain. *"I'll take it,"* thought Tony as he got dressed.

Going downstairs to the kitchen was yet another reminder of how he had slowed down, and Tony felt a mixture of sorrow and anger. Stairs were not supposed to be a challenge. He remembered running upstairs and downstairs without a thought for the activity. Racing his friends, sometimes actually winning. Climbing fences, hills, trees, whatever lay in

his path, with ease and quickness that was now forever beyond his reach except as a memory.

"Snap out of it, pal. You have work to do," Tony said out loud to himself as he reached the last step to the kitchen level. Walking was not too difficult now as he crossed the floor to the cabinets and the countertop. Breakfast was such a routine that Tony prepared his coffee, oatmeal, and fruit, banana today, almost without thought. The day was bright and sunny and would be perfect for his little project.

Tony ate his breakfast at the kitchen table, not bothering with the living room and the television. The news seemed more depressing with each passing day, and those morning talk shows were getting too ridiculous for him. Instead, he thought of his father and his uncle Bob.

Both his father and uncle had served in World War II. Uncle Bob, while not a true blood relation, was such a close friend of his father that everyone accepted him as a family member. Dad had seen action all through Europe and ended up fighting within one hundred fifty miles of Berlin at the very end of the war with the Germans. Uncle Bob had served as a marine in the Pacific, *"Island hopping like crossing a stream stone to stone,"* as he loved to say. Both had made it home and though Uncle Bob had remained a bachelor while Tony's dad married and raised Tony and his younger brother Mario, they stayed friends until the end. And as Tony and Mario grew up, they spent many a day listening to the stories of their dad and uncle.

Stories of camaraderie, pain, and suffering, but also some of the goodness in what people chose to do in terrible circumstances. Stories of how they both visited relatives of their buddies who had died to share with them their love and respect for the lost one. Of how returning a ring or an unfinished letter was received as if it were a ton of gold by distraught parents or, in one case, a young widow. Many of the stories they told resulted in tears.

Tony got up after finishing breakfast, did a few short squat exercises, and took his bowl and cup to the sink. These days, he always did his chores immediately as it seemed harder and harder to do them if he put the tasks off *"to later."* Next, off to the front porch and the work for today.

He went to the porch and grabbed the triangular display case that held the flag. It was the one given to him at his dad's funeral earlier in the year *"by a grateful nation,"* as addressed to him by the sergeant of the honor guard. He had kept it in his closet for all that time, wanting to hang it but never getting around to it. But no more. *"Today's the day,"* Tony thought or said out loud; it didn't matter. His knees announced their presence as he picked up the case, but that, too, didn't matter. Pushing the screen door open, Tony then took the two steps down to the ground level slowly and with focus.

The flagpole stood inside the raised circular enclosure, centered on a reinforced slab of cement, surrounded by a narrow circular flowerbed now filled with weeds. *"That's next,"* thought Tony as he approached. The halyard, the five-sixteenths rope used to hoist and lower the flag, was still secured tightly to the cleat and looked to be in good shape. Tony leaned forward, unraveled the halyard from the cleat, and pulled it down until the snap hooks for the flag were in position.

It was at this point where, traditionally, a second person would be available to assist, but today, Tony was alone. And since he was in no mood to ask anyone for help, he prepared to do the rest by himself. It was important to him that the flag at no point touched the ground, but Tony saw no harm in laying it out onto the bricks of the flagpole enclosure. This he did after carefully taking the flag out of the display case and gently unfolding it to expose the grommets. He then attached the two snap hooks to the corresponding grommets on the flag and, after checking the connections, stood back for a moment to review his preparations.

All seemed ready. Tony took the display case off the edge of the pole enclosure and set it on the ground. He then grabbed the halyard firmly with both hands and, with reverence, started to hoist the flag up the pole. He felt a surge of pride as he did the work, especially as he saw the flag unfurl as it rose on the flagpole. Finally, as the flag reached the top, Tony gave a few light tugs and then tied the halyard onto the cleat.

It was done. And though there was no wind at the moment, the flag still projected majesty to Tony as it hung eighteen feet up. "Finally, Dad, it is as it should be. As it should have been for a year now, I know, but there it is. And there it will stay. And for you too, Uncle Bob." Tony spoke the words to his heroes and himself as he stood on his front lawn staring at the flag. He stood there for a few minutes just looking up at it, occasionally catching a glimpse of a flutter as a slight wind gust moved the fabric, seemingly to bring the flag alive.

Finally, something told him, *"That's enough,"* and after offering the flag a civilian's salute, Tony bent to pick up the case and walk back to the house.

"Hey, sir. It's nice to see our flag flying in front of a house these days." A voice said, causing Tony to turn around. There in the street was a police car. The cop must have seen Tony raising the flag as he passed by on patrol and stopped to watch.

"Yeah, it is my father's flag, something I have been meaning to do for some time now."

"Well, it looks great. Your dad would be proud," said the cop. "Have a good day, sir. And thank you."

The policeman drove off.

Tony watched the patrol car as it departed and turned once more to gaze at the flag. Then he strolled back to the house, the display case in his hand, pain-free for the first time in a long time, a smile on his face.

Sniper Thoughts

I am alone.

I am the sniper. Even my brother and sister marines see me as different, sometimes more, mostly less than them. I am unfair.

I don't warn, feint, or show off to intimidate. My word is the final act. I show no mercy. I am invisible, undetectable, a shadow, a ghost. I am alone. My only true colleagues are others like me.

They are also alone.

They are the only others who understand my isolation…even in crowded, friendly places.

Our doctrine is different. We are charged with eliminating specific opponents for well-defined reasons. Our primary mission is to preserve the lives of our comrades-in-arms, a noble and honorable goal for anyone in the military. We are the force multipliers on a very personal level. We keep our enemies uncertain, less confident, cautious, and even scared.

Our world is stealth, rifle, scope, reticle, and trigger control. Not seen, not heard, neither before nor after our job is done.

But most don't see it that way. To them, we are just killers, marines that don't play by the rules, cheaters of a lesser morality.

Our intense training expertise in infiltration, execution, and extraction is ignored by others; they only see the moment when the shot is fired and an unsuspecting person is killed. They either fail or choose not to understand that our assigned targets are those who would either directly or indirectly cause the deaths of many on our side, maybe even the critics themselves.

No, we are looked at briefly and then ignored at parties, weddings, and gatherings of all kinds. People who know what we do cannot seem to be able to converse with us, laugh with us, or share with us in any meaningful way. They see us as killers only, a threat to everyone, an undesirable threat to all people.

And we suffer.

Isolation costs us emotionally more than anything else. My compatriots usually don't last long in the civilian world unless they continue to serve as law enforcement special operators or even mercenaries. Suicides are not uncommon among former combat snipers. There are ways to cope, but not everyone can handle the future when the past holds an intensity that is off the charts in the real world.

As for me, I have my own strategy.

My closest friends are the only ones who know the truth about me. About my role as a Scout/Sniper. As an independent warrior, a skilled shooter, and a savior to my fellow marines on the battlefield. The invisible overwatch that kept so many of them alive. And no one knows my true count. That will be my secret forever. Not even the official record is correct.

As for everyone else, I am just another former marine. Another infantry rifleman, nothing more, nothing less. I make up stories to tell when I must, several as false as they are memorized, easy off the tongue, and totally believable to my audience. Very few know the truth, and that is exactly how I want it.

I still stay in touch with some of my brethren. We meet at the range, do some plinking with civilian-purchased rifles, and laugh when we miss.

I am still in love with the concept of hitting the bullseye at any range, under any condition, with any rifle.

Especially now, since the targets are only paper and metallic silhouettes. I do my best to live in the now and not dwell on some of the things I have done for my country. Things that many years later, I can acknowledge as extreme and unpleasant. But then I realize that even now, as this is written, there are those doing and training to do the very things I did in the past. Probably, with advanced technology, I would be hard-pressed to understand, let alone utilize.

And so, I sit here, a former marine who, among many others, saw some of the horrors in the world and was lucky enough to come home afterward, physically and over time, emotionally as well.

I can finally say that I have found an inner strength that will continue to allow me to serve again as a husband, father, and a man of peace.

Full Circle

The only fan letter I ever wrote was to Johnny Winter when I was fourteen years old. He was a famous blues and rock and roll guitarist who had a unique and scratchy voice. I had purchased a few of his albums, but when a friend of mine bought me his *"Johnny Winter And Live"* album as a gift, I became an instant fan. His renditions of several songs by other artists were fantastic, and so I wrote the letter.

A few months later, while I was at school, Johnny Winter himself called my house. When my mother picked up the phone, Johnny Winter introduced himself, told her about my fan letter, and offered her two free tickets for me and a guest to see his upcoming show at the *Filmore East Theater* in New York City.

My mother knew who Johnny Winter was because I had played his records all over the house. But she was first and foremost the mother of a fourteen-year-old boy. And so, she thanked Johnny Winter, told him that I was too young to travel to New York City, and hung up.

This event was kept from me for several years.

Then, one day, while sitting around the supper table, the subject of rock and roll, concerts, and famous groups came up. One thing led to another until my mother told the story of the Johnny Winter phone call.

I was stunned. I could not believe that she did not accept the tickets that day. I pointed out that I had several older friends at the time and, beyond that, could have been escorted by an uncle or something. She said she was busy when he called and did not think of those alternatives.

I was angry with my mom for a while after that. I was disappointed that she thought me too young to travel to the city as I had secretly made several trips there with my friends at the time. And, of course, revealing that got both my parents angry at me, but as time went by, all returned to normal. By then, I had already seen Johnny Winter in concert anyway, so the significance of the phone call faded away.

Until now, that is.

As I sit here in my present situation, I cannot help but reflect on that event. My wife and I recently were granted custody of our thirteen-year-old granddaughter, Cassidy. It was the result of a horrible car accident last spring that took the lives of our son and his wife.

Since that time, we have done all we can to welcome Cassidy into our home and raise her the best we could. For all of us, the tragedy of our loss remains real and barely beneath the surface of our everyday lives. Things are slowly improving.

And herein lies the dilemma. A few days ago, Cassidy came home from school all excited. It seems her girlfriend, Joanna, was notified that she had won a contest and had been awarded two tickets to see Miley Cyrus next month in Philadelphia at the Academy of Music. As she and Cassidy are best friends, Joanna invited Cassidy to go with her to the concert.

The logistics are no worries. They could take a train from Newark directly to and from Philadelphia with only a short walk to the venue from the train station. Money is no problem, either. The obvious concern is that they would be two young girls on their own in a large city. Clearly, Cassidy needs our permission to go, and part of me is grateful that she thought enough of us to ask. But what to do?

What would you do?

Swim Call

The sea was calm, a light blue expanse that extended to the horizon in all directions with only a hint of mild wave motion, a tranquil sight.

Suddenly and without warning, a long, thin black metal tube rose up into the air, trailing a wake of white water as it moved. It continued upward only to stop its rise at about ten feet above the surface. The glass aperture at its top rotated clockwise through two complete circles. After an exposure of less than ten seconds, the periscope dropped back beneath the water.

About two minutes later, the submarine surfaced smoothly and without a sound. Where there had been only ocean before, now floated one of the world's most powerful weapons, a United States Navy nuclear fast attack submarine.

The boat continued moving forward at a slow speed but, after a few minutes, came to a complete stop. And by that time, the sail of the sub was already occupied. Several sailors now stood on the enclosed watch station area, and others stood above and behind them along with the masts themselves. Some had binoculars, and one was armed with a machine gun.

But for Alan McGovern, the surfacing maneuver was just another part of his busy day, and he was isolated from the activity above. It was midsummer of 2007, and McGovern was a nuclear electrician's mate aboard the *USS Albuquerque*, now assigned to the Southern Command.

They were operating in the Caribbean Sea, somewhat northeast of Aruba, in deep water and had recently completed more than two intense weeks of wartime drills. McGovern had been on board for a little over a year and was fully qualified. That is, he had earned his dolphin pin and was, therefore, considered a viable part of the crew.

McGovern, also known as Mac, was assigned as throttle man, a critical asset in that he controlled the speed of the boat. As a throttle man, Mac was one of the few crew members stationed in Maneuvering, the control center for the engineering spaces in the back, or aft, end of the submarine.

His job was to first acknowledge the speed order from the Main Control Room and then to match the ordered speed to the actual speed by way of either opening or shutting the throttle valve, basically, a giant wheel. Progress was measured by watching a gauge, which showed a yellow arrow that indicated the assigned speed, and a red arrow that showed the actual speed of the sub. How smoothly and quickly a throttle man matched the two arrows on the gauge without causing cavitation was the true measure of how efficient he was.

Mac, with only a relatively short time on the Albuquerque, was the best. He was well known for his quick reaction time and was already responsible for setting a record on board the submarine. He had proven so good that he was assigned as throttle man not only at his watch station but during general quarters as well.

On this occasion, he was ordered to slow first to ahead one-third, then to full stop. Normally, those in maneuvering did not have a need to know why the submarine changed speed, but this time around, everyone knew the reason. And it was a good one.

Swim call.

Swim call was a luxury, especially for a submarine crew, that was reserved as a reward for only the best performance during a mission. The assemblage of sailors on a submarine is always a mix of experienced submariners, those with a few years of experience, and those relatively new to the world of undersea Navy life. Those not yet qualified on all the boat's systems were referred to as NUBs, non-useful bodies, and were treated with near contempt.

It is, therefore, the combination of leadership, experience, talent, relentless training, and follow-through that turns such a group into a solid crew. And even though the submarine community is drawn from only the best navy candidates, there is still much room for development. As it was, the crew of the *USS Albuquerque* were at their best.

In the past two weeks, the navy threw all they could at the submarine in the form of drills and challenges. A fleet of ships and aircraft was sent out to seek and destroy the boat in an aggressive anti-submarine style. The sub was tasked with evading all threats as well as detecting, tracking, and attacking everything from tankers to cruisers. They were directed to conduct unexpected emergency-deep drills, snapshot torpedo launches, and address jam dive casualties. As far as engineering casualties were concerned, everything from a diesel fuel fire to a reactor scram was covered, sometimes repeatedly.

In all cases, the Albuquerque crew performed well, demonstrating a very high-efficiency rating and, on a few occasions, breaking existing records. And the officers and the enlisted alike knew it. Most significantly, the captain knew it. And so, swim call became the order of the day.

Once the submarine had surfaced and the area was secured, with no other vessel in sight, the long-awaited *"Swim call, now, swim call"* was announced over the IMC. Much of the crew, not currently on the watch or stuck with essential duties, then started to appear topside by way of the forward hatch. The swim call took place off the starboard side and not further aft than amidships.

No one was allowed near the reactor compartment, even on the outside of the sub, due to the ever-present increased radiation level. Marker buoys were set out to define the limit alongside the boat. The crew was advised not to swim further out than fifty yards from the sub, and both divers were assigned as lifeguards.

And it was great. They were in the tropics, and the water temperature was in the eighties. The water itself seemed crystal clear, and the only things that made some of the crew nervous were the fact that the water at this location was more than a mile deep, there was no five-foot swimming pool here, and, of course, the threat of sharks. One guard with a gun, even a machine gun, didn't seem like enough protection for many people, so they stayed close, hanging onto the rope ladders or the netting laid down the hull.

But there were a few brave souls among the crew. A few who were good swimmers took off and swam out and away from the boat. Many had to be called back in by the megaphone-equipped *"sail guards"* as they challenged the perimeter. But overall, the swim call was a rousing success, bringing forth a level of high morale not seen in quite a while.

At one point, one of the sail guards thought he saw a shark's fin approaching those in the water. As he looked again, he noticed that there were many fins, not just one, and they were heading swiftly toward the swimmers.

But then, and to his great relief, he realized they were dolphins, not sharks. And what happened next was one of those rare occurrences, a miraculous rarity, and an event that would never be forgotten.

The swim call had been scheduled to start no later than 1000 and end around 1400. This was to allow even those who stood the morning and afternoon watches to have at least a couple of hours to swim if they wanted to.

McGovern had been one of those standing the morning watch, and so, at about 1230, he appeared on deck to take his turn in the water. Not only was Mac a good swimmer, but he also loved diving. And so, after a short time swimming around, he decided to try a few dives off the starboard fair-weather plane. Others had the same idea, and Mac had to wait a while for his turn. When it came, he was ready. But in his haste, he made a classic and very dumb mistake. He failed to look down prior to his dive and check to see if the coast was clear. It was not.

As McGovern left the platform, only then did he notice someone swimming below, someone who should not have been there but was. They collided a second later. Jacobs was hit high on the shoulder and was pushed mostly to the side rather than underwater, but McGovern hit Jacobs a glancing blow with his head and was immediately knocked out. One of the divers had seen the accident as it occurred and rushed to dive in to save Jacobs. But since Mac had much more downward momentum, he continued to travel deeper underwater even after the collision and was temporarily lost to sight.

Some of the others already in the water had also seen part or all of the accident, but no one was quick enough to dive down after the now unconscious throttle man. By this time, the second diver, Klausner, had moved up to the area of the hull beneath the plane and was frantically searching for a sign of McGovern so he could go get him, but he did not yet have a fix on Mac's location. He did, however, notice the dolphins.

The dolphins had been hanging around the submarine since shortly after it surfaced. For the most part, they stayed away, just happy to be in the area. On a few occasions, one or two of the dolphins would approach a swimming sailor, then quickly swim away. There was no cause for alarm. Indeed, all were glad to have the dolphins around. *"Where dolphins, no sharks"* was a phrase all sailors knew. But what happened next was amazing.

Shortly after the collision, and just as McGovern started to sink, two of the dolphins rushed in. One stayed near the surface while the other dove down. A few seconds later, Klausner spotted McGovern being pushed up to the surface by the dolphin. He did not hesitate and dove in to rescue his still-unconscious shipmate. The dolphin on the surface swam up to Klausner and allowed him to grab its dorsal fin. The dolphin then towed the amazed diver toward Mac much faster than he could have swum the distance himself. In the meantime, the first dolphin was doing its best to push McGovern toward the approaching diver.

Finally, upon reaching Mac, Klausner quickly assessed that he was still breathing and grabbed him to tow him back to the sub. But dolphin number two was not done yet. It quickly positioned itself to allow Klausner to grab onto its dorsal fin once again. And once again, the dolphin towed Klausner, with Mac firmly held, this time to the submarine.

Many hands helped both sailors up onto the deck. By now, McGovern had regained consciousness, though still a little groggy. But it was a miracle that he was alive at all. And the reason?

The dolphins.

Some of the sailors had continued to watch the dolphins throughout the entire episode, so it was witnessed that the two involved did a few flying leaps as they departed.

The two injured crewmen were quickly taken to sick bay and eventually improved well enough to return to full duty. Diving off the fair-weather planes was secured. And for the remaining swim call, everyone was understandably more cautious. But the word quickly spread throughout the submarine and eventually much further of the encounter with the dolphins and how they had helped a near-drowning submariner. And it was yet again reaffirmed why the symbol pin of the submarine service is two dolphins swimming alongside a submarine.

Cousins

"Gordon, is that you?" Eric shouted as he approached what looked to be his cousin.

"Yes. Over here," Gordon responded, happy that they were able to find each other among so many others.

They met up next to a small grove of trees on the hill just below the last gentle slope to the crest. Each man leaned his rifle against one of the trees and, after greeting each other with handshakes and back slaps, sat down. Eric had two small leafy branches in his hand and, as the two men settled in, handed one of them to his cousin.

"What's this?" Gordon asked.

"A sprig of mint for you. I found it down the hill by the stream, not far from our line. I thought you would like it. I always find mint refreshing."

"Yeah, me too. Thanks." Gordon broke off a couple of leaves and put them in his mouth. The sharp tang of the mint burst with flavor after a couple of chews and was indeed pleasant, bringing a smile to Gordon's face.

"How is everyone back in Pittsburgh?" asked Gordon of his cousin.

"They are well. My dad got a promotion at the factory about six months ago and was finally able to put a down payment on a house. He misses the family, especially your mom, and wanted me to pass on his best wishes if I ever got the chance to see her."

"Mom is fine, and our farm is doing well. Looks like another good crop for us, and hopefully, we will be able to purchase some more acreage for next year. I don't know if you are aware, but she birthed a baby just last month, my baby brother Tom. Everyone is doing fine. Please tell your family the good news." Gordon retrieved his canteen, took a long pull, and offered it to Eric. Eric accepted, took a modest drink, and handed the canteen back to Gordon.

The late morning breeze swept across the hillside, creating a moving wave effect on the long grass. It was a nice day with a deep blue sky and a few puffy white clouds drifting to the east. Birds had returned to the area, and the sounds of their chirping and calls added to the sense of peace.

The two young men had always enjoyed each other's company, and today was no exception. They had not seen each other for nearly a year and never before under such circumstances, but none of that mattered at the moment. There was much to share, and share they did. Life for both of their families had been very busy in recent times, and both Eric and Gordon enjoyed the opportunity to speak of their kinfolk back home. Both families were prospering in spite of the difficult times, and neither had yet suffered loss or tragedy.

"Whatever happened to Rosemary, your older sister?" Gordon asked.

"Oh, she did well. She is married to a professor at the Western Pennsylvania Medical College," said Eric. "No children yet, but then again, who knows?"

Both men shared a brief laugh at that.

After a few more comfortable exchanges, the cousins lay back in the grass beneath the shade of the trees, alone with their thoughts. The world in those moments seemed a perfect place. After a while, Eric spoke up again.

"Do you think we will ever get out of this mess, Gordon?"

"I don't know, but I wish we could all just go home," Gordon replied. "I am so tired of it all."

At that moment, a bugle blast, long and demanding and originating from the hilltop, broke the quiet of the day. Soon after, another bugle blast sounded its summons, this one from down the hill and near the stream. Both men arose from their rest and, without a word, embraced each other in a long fraternal hug. It was again Eric who spoke first.

"Be careful out there, my cousin, my kin. And do me a favor."

"Anything," said Gordon, fighting back tears.

"When you go back, angle off to the right. I will do the same when I go," said Eric. "I just can't stand the thought of us actually firing at each other. Okay?"

"Yes. I understand," Gordon said. "Goodbye, Eric. Hope to see you again soon."

And with that, after grabbing their rifles, the two men, the two cousins, parted. Eric walked down the hill along with many others to his garrison of Union troops. And Gordon went uphill toward the line with his fellow Confederate soldiers.

The brief truce had ended, and the business of war was about to resume.

Porch Chair

Cori had a beautiful porch chair. It was made of wicker and featured a wide seat, a lofty back, and two armrests. A soft pillow on the seat made it a very comfortable piece of furniture.

The chair sat on the far-right side of Cori's front porch. There was a little extra space to the right of the chair for a small table and, on the left side, a comfortable amount of room that allowed Cori to rise from her chair and take a few steps before entering her house.

Cori's house sat on a corner in the town of Bixby where two lightly trafficked streets met up. The first, Elm Street, approached her home from the front left and, after making a sharp left turn, became Bremmer Street.

Both were well tree'd and presented a much more relaxing mood than the main thoroughfare of Hulslander Avenue a few blocks away. What made Cori's neighborhood especially nice, however, was the fact that her property was adjacent to Comiskey Park, part of the largest of the town's park system, green, peaceful, and protected.

In her younger years, Cori was an avid hiker. She and her friends would travel all around, sometimes even out of state, to seek out new and remote trails. Cori had worn out quite a few pairs of hiking shoes in her day and had several photo albums full of pictures from her years of adventure. But several years ago, it had all come to an end as she suffered a badly broken leg on a fall during a hike at Harriman State Park in New York.

She spent months in recovery and, true to her doctor's prediction, had not been able to walk comfortably since. Physical therapy, aggressive and specific gym workouts, high energy supplements; nothing was able to return Cori to the hiker she once was. Her pain was controlled somewhat by over-the-counter medications only. Cori refused anything stronger for fear of becoming dependent.

And so, the porch and the nearby park became the most significant things in Cori's life. She still had a handful of friends that she would occasionally get together with and a significant stock portfolio that granted her financial independence. But Cori ended up spending a lot of time alone. She never married; her parents were deceased, and her sister lived far away in South Dakota.

But despite this, Cori lived a full life. Her hobbies included cooking, and she had a contract with a cooking magazine that had her writing two articles a month. Her local church was the lucky recipient of most of the things Cori cooked, but she ate a fair amount of her creations herself. Over the years, the inevitable occurred, and Cori, now in her sixties, had gained a few extra pounds.

It was, therefore, daily walks in the park that became one of Cori's main activities. She would take her time, most often bring her cane, and trek through some of the many trails that passed through Comiskey Park. She took advantage of the many benches that dotted the trails, and often, her walks took Cori away from her home for several hours.

Upon her return one day, Cori was startled to notice her front door was open even though the outer porch door was closed. Thinking she had just forgotten to close her front door, Cori went up her porch stairs and entered her home. It was a mistake.

As she passed through her living room and started toward the kitchen, Cori was grabbed from behind and roughly thrown to the floor. The two men who had been ransacking her home then placed Cori in a kitchen chair and secured her to it using duct tape. She was then muzzled, again with duct tape, and blindfolded with one of her kitchen towels.

"We are almost done. If you stay quiet and don't try to escape, you will not be harmed," a rough and very scary voice said in her ear. "But try anything stupid, and you will be hurt. Get it?" Cori shook her head yes and, as scared as she was, decided just to ride it out.

The robbers left a few minutes later. Cori then started to struggle with her bindings to escape so she could call the police. As it happened, however, it took her several hours to wriggle loose from the duct tape that had her bound up, and it was after nightfall before she was able to get help.

During the ensuing investigation, it was discovered that besides some cash and jewelry, the robbers had not taken many things that couldn't be replaced or that Cori herself cared that much about. The house was dusted for fingerprints, and the detectives gave her advice on home security issues, but in the end, Cori was once again alone.

However, this event really shook her up. Over the next few weeks, Cori found she had trouble sleeping. She remained worried that these robbers would come back. Even her porch-sitting became more of a sentry position than just a place to relax. She did take precautions suggested by the detectives. She always kept her doors locked. She kept her shades down. And she paid more attention to what people looked like and what they were wearing.

But it didn't seem to be enough. So, finally, one day, Cori went up to her attic and retrieved the .45 pistol her uncle had carried with him in Vietnam. He had given it to Cori some years ago, showed her how to use it, how to load and unload it, and even brought her to a range for some live fire practice. Even though Cori had been scared of the gun, she allowed her uncle to take her through the training. But since those few days, the gun had remained up in Cori's attic, untouched and forgotten.

Until today.

Cori brought the pistol down to the living room and checked it out. It was heavier than she had remembered it to be. She released the magazine, noticed it was full, and returned it to the gun, a loud click telling her it had locked into place. She thought she was finally ready, so Cori placed the gun in the right-side pocket of her dress and went out to sit on the porch chair.

At first, the added weight of the gun felt awkward, but as time went by, Cori got used to the routine of arming herself before sitting on the porch. It did make her feel more secure, and she told herself it would only be used to defend herself. Cori never brought the gun along when she took her walks in the park and kept it in her lamp table drawer in the house whenever she was not in her porch chair. Things eventually got back to normal for her.

Billy Shellhammer worked in the Walmart along Hulslander Avenue in the downtown section of Bixby. He had been there for many years and was now one of the store managers at that location. He lived alone since his wife had passed away and was sixty-one years old.

In his position, Billy often had to work extended hours, so at the end of his shift, the last thing he needed was a long, frustrating drive home through the horrendous traffic on Hulslander Avenue. And so, he found a shortcut, an alternate route that saved him up to fifteen minutes for his trips home. A quick right turn down Elm Street off of Hulslander, followed by a looping left onto Bremmer Street, was just the right medicine to allow Billy to enjoy some of his drive home. The tree-lined roads did much to relax his mind and shake off the day.

It was during such rides that Billy noticed the home just on the corner of Elm and Bremmer, in particular, the large wicker chair that occupied the corner of the home's front porch. It was set in a perfect position to oversee the traffic coming down Elm Street and to observe the woodsy entrance to Comiskey Park. Most of the time, the chair was empty, but on a few occasions, Billy noticed a woman sitting in the chair. She looked about his age and, though a little heavy-set, was attractive to his eyes.

But, as his attention was on making the left turn from Elm to Bremmer without getting into an accident, his observation time was quite limited. Nonetheless, over time, a curiosity about this woman in the porch chair started building in Billy's mind. And in spite of a basic shyness in his personal life, Billy came up with a plan to someday meet this lady and talk with her.

Working at Walmart helped. Billy was easily able to purchase a small cooler and a variety of drinks, such as iced tea, lemonade, and a few sodas. He even threw in a couple of beers. His plan was to wait until he saw the lady on her porch, pull over, and approach her with the cooler, offering her a drink of her choice and, therefore, break the ice to start a conversation. It was a bold move for him, Billy knew, but after so many occasions of seeing this lady in her porch chair, he figured he had to do something. And so, each day during his lunch break, Billy would purchase some ice and replace the water from yesterday's ice in the cooler, just to ensure cold drinks in case this was to be the day he saw the woman on the porch.

Finally, on a warm Friday afternoon, all things came together for Billy. It was a very light traffic day on Elm, and as he approached the corner, he saw the lady sitting in her porch chair. Sure enough, there was a parking spot right in front of the house, so Billy pulled over and parked. He reached over, grabbed the cooler off the passenger seat, and got out of the car. He then crossed over the small sidewalk and approached the woman's front porch, smiling and waving as he did so.

"Hello there," Billy said by way of greeting.

Cori had noticed the entire sequence of events. She even recognized the car and driver as she had seen him passing her house on many occasions. Though that in and of itself was not too extraordinary, it did cause her to become cautious. And now this. The man had pulled over and was coming onto her lawn, heading directly for her. Memories of her encounter with the two robbers came to her, and in spite of his seemingly pleasant demeanor, Cori was suddenly afraid of this man. And he was not hesitating. He was actually starting to climb the porch stairs, coming right for her.

Cori pulled the gun from her dress pocket and shot the man.

Except she didn't.

The gun did not fire. Cori, though setting the magazine into the .45, had not engaged the weapon's slide to put a bullet into the firing chamber, nor had she cocked the hammer. When she pulled the trigger, nothing happened. But Cori, though surprised, still kept the gun pointed at the man. And that was certainly enough for Billy.

"Don't shoot, lady, please don't shoot!" Billy stammered as he started backtracking off the stairs, nearly falling off the porch. Somehow, he managed not to drop the cooler and put his free hand up to try to ward off this sudden threat.

"What are you doing here?" Cori yelled. "Are you trying to rob me?" Cori's trembling hand kept the pistol up even as she started to have doubts about this entire situation.

"No. No. I just wanted to offer you a drink from my cooler here. Please, please put the gun down. I mean you no harm." Billy could not seem to get the words out fast enough.

Cori, now realizing the magnitude of her mistake, quickly returned the pistol to her pocket and, in a much different tone, said, "I am so sorry. I don't know you. I thought you were attacking me. Who are you?"

"I am Billy, Billy Shellhammer. I work at the Walmart on Hulslander, right down the road. I have seen you in your chair many times over the past few years, and I just wanted to meet you, that's all. Damn lady, you scared the crap out of me!"

I am so sorry," Cori said again. "My name is Cori. Cori Clarkson. Please forgive me. I was quite scared myself. Please come up. Can we start over?"

"Yeah, sure, if you promise not to shoot me, that is." Billy tried for humor even as he struggled to calm down.

"Okay, okay. The damn thing doesn't work anyway. Thank God." Cori responded.

With that, Billy took the four steps onto the porch and had his first chat with Cori. She told him of the break-in and her captivity by the two home invaders still less than a year ago. That went a long way to get Billy to at least understand why Cori reacted to him in the way she did. As it turned out, they had all the drinks in the cooler, including the two beers. Cori sat in her porch chair, and Billy sat on the porch railing in front of her. Their conversation went well, and they agreed to see each other again.

When Billy left, Cori called the police, not against Billy, but to say she found an old gun in her attic and wanted them to come and pick it up as she didn't want guns in her house. Over time, she and Billy grew closer and closer. He loved her cooking. They took long, thoughtful walks in the park and, within a year, decided to marry. And as far as this tale goes, they did indeed live happily ever after.

Part Two:
Science Fiction

Traveling Through Torrey Pines

The Old Ones thought that the magic was in the place. That may be correct, but it is not the end of it. I believe the magic is also in the trees. I know this to be true because I purchased a sapling from the park, brought it back to New Jersey, and planted it in my yard. After only ten years or so, my Torrey Pine tree is already showing me things.

Let me explain…

Several years ago, while in our forties, my wife Susan and I took a vacation to San Diego, California. During our stay, the two of us decided to enjoy a relaxing day away from the city and in one of the area's many state parks. Torrey Pines State Park looked like a suitable place and was not far away. According to our hotel brochure, it was located along the coast and featured everything from beaches to cliffs to many winding trails with views of the ocean. It seemed perfect for us, and we both shared a good feeling about the day trip.

Oh yes…feelings.

Sue and I both share a special gift. Some would call it clairvoyance or a psychic twinkle, but we don't go that far. To us, it is nothing more than an extra, enhanced ability to detect the feelings of each other and other people as well, sometimes as they are just developing. It helps tremendously in avoiding conflicts.

In addition, we each have the ability, on occasion, to sense when something is about to happen, usually something personal and close by. Again, nothing amazing like knowing a winning lottery number or who will win a sporting event, but things that allow us to avoid accidents, wrong turns, and, in general, bad outcomes. Over the years, we have come to terms with our gifts and calmly accepted them as part of our lives.

At the entrance to the park, we had a chance to talk with one of the park rangers. It was soon after the park opened, and there was no one else around. He told us that the Torrey Pine was known to grow only in this area and on a few small islands offshore. He explained that the original inhabitants of this park were the Toreros, an offshoot of the larger Diegueno tribe and that they believed that this was a magical place where some people could see many wonderful things.

"Is there any danger here?" Susan asked as we both felt there might be something more.

"Well, you do have to be careful along the trails. Sometimes they take you close to some drop-offs, and the sandy soil can be loose," was his response, "but nothing out of the ordinary." He must have sensed something about us because he then added. "Just don't believe everything you see." That seemed odd, but just then, another car pulled up behind us, and the ranger waved us on.

We drove on up the park road as it wound up a hilly area with many sharp turns. The scenery was a mix of low shrubs and light soil, rocky in some places and with several types of trees all around. Finally, the terrain leveled off, and soon after, we saw the parking lots that surrounded the Visitor's Center. I parked the car, and we went in.

The facility had all the usual things: books, leaflets, maps, all kinds of souvenirs, and even displays of the animals and birds that inhabited the area. Several posters of the Torrey Pine were also available, as well as saplings of the tree itself. Sue and I ended up buying a map of the park as well as one of the saplings. We were warned that the tree is often difficult to grow in areas that differ from the park, but we took one anyway.

After leaving the Visitor's Center, we decided to start our hike from a trail that began from the parking lot not far from our car. The trail started off going on level terrain, dense with shrubs and trees, but quickly opened to the general park layout.

Torrey Pines State Park is situated in an area where the sloping mountains drop off to the Pacific Ocean. There is much evidence of wind and especially water erosion throughout the land as deep channels and canyons seem to be everywhere mixed in with the hills, all ending up on the beaches far below. As we walked the trail, Sue and I could see that in some areas, guard rails had been erected where the pathway passed close to a steep drop-off in the terrain. But, for the most part, the trail was easy to navigate and intersected with many other trails as we walked along.

At one point, we stopped for a detailed look at one of the pine trees that made this park unique. Right away, we saw that the tree had a more open crown design than the pine trees we were used to seeing in the east. Independent and thick branches came off the main trunk and gave the tree a lofty appearance. The pine needles were the longest we had ever seen, and they grew in clusters of five. The roots that we could see seemed thicker than those of pine trees we were familiar with, but the overall presentation of the Torrey pine was one of elegance. We took several pictures.

The hike along the trail was pleasant, more of a stroll since there was no rush. As we looked downhill, we could see several trails with a few other people walking along them. Soon after we started, we came upon a well-manicured bench, so we took a seat and just settled back to watch the goings-on. We were facing the ocean, looking down upon a beautiful landscape with a warm sun overhead and the sea breeze in our faces; it was wonderful.

"Hey, look at that," Sue said, pointing to another trail down below us.

I looked down to the right and saw what she meant. A couple was walking along one of the trails, and at first glance, I saw nothing odd. But as I continued to watch, I noticed a few strange details. The man was dressed in a black suit and wearing a top hat, low cut, but a top hat, nonetheless. And the lady was wearing a long dress that nearly touched the ground. She was carrying a flowered and laced parasol over her left shoulder. They were dressed in the style of the early twentieth century.

"That's strange," I said to Sue. "They must be dressed for a movie or something. Actors on a break?"

As we continued to watch, the pair went behind a small grove of trees and shrubs. We waited for them to emerge out the other side, but they didn't, even after several minutes. Curious now, Sue and I decided to hike down to the spot and see where they went.

Getting to the location took a few minutes since our trail took us parallel for a while before joining with the trail the others had been on, but soon enough, we arrived at the place alongside the group of trees that had earlier blocked our view. But there, the mystery deepened. There was no other trail at that spot, not even a bench where they might have taken a seat for a rest, as we had just done.

So, where had they gone?

We looked around for a while but discovered no answer. Soon after, we continued our hike, but the feeling tone for us had changed.

About a half hour later, we had traveled further out into the park and a little more downhill. The ocean was still quite a way below us, but we had dropped down about one hundred feet from the parking lot level. Between the ever-warming sun and the hiking, Sue and I both needed a rest and some water, so at the next available bench, we again took a seat. We each took a water bottle from our waistpacks and just sat and sipped for a while, once again enjoying the view. There were a few more people walking the trails by now, but nothing out of the ordinary.

Then we saw the cowboys. There were three of them, two men and a boy. All were dressed cowboy style, complete with dusty jeans, bandanas around their necks, and Stetson-like hats on their heads. The two men even had guns in holsters at their hips. The boy, though unarmed, nonetheless had that rough and tumble demeanor of the two men.

That, in and of itself, was strange enough. It was yet another sighting that seemed out of place in this quiet and peaceful setting. And what followed convinced both of us that there was something extraordinary going on here.

The three cowboys were walking along the trail, about thirty yards downhill from us and very nearly in front of where we were sitting. They were moving along at a steady pace, in no apparent hurry, and seemed relaxed. We could hear that the man in the back was saying something, but we could not make out the words.

But as they continued to walk, something happened. All three, at the same time, seemed to slowly start to fade away. They became thinner and thinner, more transparent at each step, until they were gone… disappeared in the morning sun! *As if they had never been there at all!*

"Did you see that?" I said to Sue, keeping my eyes on the trail where the cowboys had vanished.

"Yes, I did," she replied, adding, "and I will bet that is just what happened to the others we saw earlier. That would explain why we never found them." Susan always had a quick, analytical mind.

"Okay, but where did they go?" I still had a few questions. And Sue, of course, was on the same wavelength with me. In the lead, as it turned out.

"How about, where did they come from? Or better yet, when did they come from?"

"What do you mean?" I said, not sure where she was coming from.

"Well, you know the theories of time displacement, right? The notion that things, even people, can travel through time either on purpose or just by a fluke of nature."

"Yeah…so what?" I was not as imaginative about such things as my wife.

"Perhaps this is what we are seeing here. Visions of people from the past who lived here and have somehow been temporarily transported through time. Maybe they don't or didn't even notice. Ha! Maybe We are making an appearance to someone in the future, someone sitting on a bench uphill from us."

"You are nuts, lady," I said, laughing. "I just wanted to go on a day hike in a California park, and you have got us traveling through time. What did you have with your breakfast this morning? That's what I want to know." I tried for a joke, but Susan was determined to make her point.

"No, seriously," Sue replied. "What if this is the explanation, the magic of the natives that the ranger was talking about? He seemed to pick up our thing back at the entrance…that is probably why he said, "Don't believe everything you see," remember?" Maybe this time displacement thing is the magic, and maybe it only happens here, and maybe it is only something that we gifted people can even witness."

As logical as it all sounded, I still had my doubts. And my feelings of the *"wonder of it all"* had definitely faded. All of a sudden, I wanted to leave this place, just get back to the car and go.

Go, go, go.

Sue felt that and stood up. "Come on, Ted, let's head back to San Diego. I will go first."

With that, we headed back. It wasn't long before I realized heading uphill on loose sandy soil was a bit more difficult than gently strolling downhill, and I soon began falling behind Sue. When she started to slow down to wait, I waved my hand and told her to keep going and that I would catch up. And so, she eventually moved out of sight. In doing so, she missed my last encounter with the magic of Torrey Pines State Park.

I had finished a turn in the trail and broke out into a relatively flat, straight section and was getting an uneasy feeling. Suddenly, as gradually as the cowboys had faded, I saw a native become visible, running directly toward me on the path. He was young and looked strong, dressed in buckskin leggings, loincloth, and leather moccasins. His upper body, though bare, was crisscrossed with streaks of black, yellow, and red paint, and in his hand, he carried a compressed bow and three arrows. He was looking ahead, but as he approached, his eyes failed to show any recognition of me.

Then, we had a pass-through. The native, in his continued running, passed right through me…through and out. He never hesitated. Soon after the encounter, as I turned to look at him, he faded away, and I was once again alone on the trail. I doubt if he ever noticed me.

But, during the pass-through, something else happened. Facts about this individual were somehow implanted into my mind. With sudden clarity, I knew him to be Haawka, a brave of his tribe who had lived through twenty-eight rainy seasons. He was joined and was a proud father of two sons. His mission on this day was hunting, to bring back a deer not only to feed his family but to help feed the tribe. He had noticed a small herd earlier and was running to catch up. Others were closing in from different directions.

In a flash, the episode came to an end, and I once more became a simple hiker on a trail. That was fine with me as now, more than ever, I just wanted out. The sun seemed a bit oppressive, and I slowly plodded along uphill until I finally reached the level area near the parking lot. I felt tired in many ways but cheered up a little when I saw Sue relaxed and leaning on our car.

"What happened?" she asked as I approached.

"Let's go, and I will tell you," was my response.

On our way out of the park, with Sue now at the wheel, I told her about the pass-through incident.

"Did you feel a chill or anything during the encounter?" she asked.

"No, nothing but that input of knowledge. I guess there is more to these episodes than just seeing things. Do you think other people have had similar experiences?"

"Well, there would have been reports or news stories or something," Sue pondered a moment, then continued, "I have an idea. Let's talk to the ranger again."

And so, we did. It had not been too long since we had entered the park, and lucky for us, the same ranger was at the gate when we approached to leave. We did not want to give too much away, but we asked him what he meant in his earlier comment. His response was interesting.

"I am a descendant of those that once inhabited this area. I don't know why, but I had a feeling that you two had a little magic in you. And…well, magic attracts magic, so I thought you would be among those that got the little extra out of this place." His eyes widened, and he said, "And you did, didn't you!"

"We sure did," said Sue, "This is a very interesting place." With that, we said goodbye, and she drove us out of there.

The rest of our trip was much less eventful, and as soon as we got home, I did the research and planted our Torrey Pine sapling in the yard. I must have done things correctly because the tree grew fast and large very quickly. Taking care of the tree as it grew became somewhat of a hobby, certainly more than a chore, and as the years went by, I became very proud of the tree. It was a unique feature in our neighborhood.

Then, one day, not long ago, we got a surprise. Sue and I were sitting in the yard not far from Torrey, as we had come to call it, when we both had a vision. Just beyond the tree was a wide expanse of flat land with other trees and bushes. Off in the distance was a dirt road, and on it, a horse and buggy rig was on the move. But there were no other houses. Beyond the road was just woods. Though confused for a moment, we both came to realize that this was a view of our own home grounds from what it must have been like over a hundred years ago!

The vision only lasted a few seconds and faded away in the same fashion as those in the state park had done many years ago. Sue and I remained outside near the tree for several hours, but the image did not recur. But we do expect more such visions in the future.

One thing is for sure.

The magic is here!

In us.

And in the Torrey Pines.

The Rock

The rock stood in front of the house from the day we moved in some fourteen years ago. It sat on the right side of the front lawn, about twenty feet in front of our enclosed front porch and about fifteen feet from the sidewalk. Its location evenly split the distance between the pathway from the porch with the driveway next to the house.

Surrounding the rock was a ring of old reddish-brown bricks that gave it the appearance of something special. It was indeed an attractive contrast to the green grass of the lawn. But to me, it was always a rock until that fateful night.

My dad is a fireman. It is a great job that he loves, and from the start, it was a good fit for him. After only a few years on the job, my father knew he had found his career, and for him, the next logical step was to move Mom, me, and my younger brother Jimmy out of the apartment and into a real house. He and Mom had been saving as much money as possible, and it turned out that he had enough for a down payment and, more importantly, earned enough to afford a twenty-year mortgage. And so, at only four years old, I moved for the first time.

It was great in that house. I had my own room. Jimmy had his, too. Our rooms were on the second floor in front. Jimmy's was on the left side, and mine was on the right. Each was above and behind the roof of the front porch, mine on the side nearest the rock. We had a nice-sized backyard with only a very slight downward slope away from the house. Dad thought that was really important for some reason.

A huge cherry tree stood along the left boundary of our yard, across from the garage, presenting us with blossoms and even cherries during the spring and summer. After a few years, Dad and Uncle Bob constructed a huge cement slab patio that extended from the back of the house out about fifteen feet into the yard. A picnic table, several lounge chairs, and even a barbeque followed. The pool didn't arrive until I was twelve.

Most of our activities in those years were close to the house, at first, only in the backyard. But as time went by and Jimmy and I grew older, we started venturing out. We met up with our friends and played boxball and touch football in the streets. Ran around with sticks at first, then toy guns, playing Army. There was even a roller skating phase. In the winter, it was time for snowmen, forts, and daily snowball fights. There were few fences between properties in those days, and our neighbors didn't seem to mind us running through yards and between homes on our adventures.

And through it all, the rock stood on our lawn, reclining really. It was a huge thing, especially in those little-kid years. It stood nearly three feet tall at its highest point, with no ragged edges. About six feet long and over half that wide, it rested on the ground, solidly attached to the earth.

There were a few patches of encrusted dirt on it with moss and even small plants growing out, but for the most part, it was bare. Though not smooth in the usual sense, the rock reminded me of a pebble you might find at the bottom of a creek. This was the granddaddy of all pebbles, to be sure. On occasion, over the years, some of us would climb up onto the rock to pretend we were king of the hill or something, but for the most part, the rock was ignored except as a landmark.

At one point, as I grew older, I developed a curiosity about the rock. *Where did it come from? Why was it here?*

By this time, I knew how to research things, so I went to the town hall and was able to trace the construction of our neighborhood. It seemed our home was part of a massive construction surge in the years following World War II. While the woodsy area across our street remained untouched, on our side was a row of homes that extended hundreds of yards off the main boulevard. The woods had been razed to the ground all along the site to provide for the construction, except for a few trees and rocks left behind as decorations for the houses. And it seemed our rock was one of the natural structures allowed to remain. A quick side note in the account mentioned that the builder had one of his masons place the red brick enclosure around our rock to ensure no one moved it. And that was fine with me. Though it was just a huge rock, the thing did add a little spice to the curb appeal of our house.

As time went on, and first bicycles, then cars took us further from our neighborhood, the rock faded in importance. It became one of those things so familiar that it was ignored, like other landscaped features. And so, as changes to the rock must have occurred prior to that nighttime event, they were never noticed.

(The dragon knew its time had come. For a time beyond measure, it had grown both in size and awareness inside the egg. Racial memories and instinct brought an understanding and a sense of its obligations to its kind in such a hostile world and what to do to ensure its survival both as an individual and a rare representative of its species. First, it had to break out of the egg that had sustained it for all these years. It was aware of the close proximity of a human family and others as well. It had even picked up enough to have a basic understanding of the human language and mannerisms. It knew of its level of exposure and that its hatching had to occur as quietly as possible. And if discovered, then steps would have to be taken to ensure its existence remained a secret).

Last Wednesday night, at about two in the morning, I heard a sound from outside my window. It was something like a snap or a crack. I lay there between awake and asleep, but the sound did not repeat. That is, just until I started to fade out again. *Crack!* There it was again. No doubt this time. It sounded like it was coming from the rock.

I rolled out of bed, threw on pants, shirt, and slippers, and quietly went downstairs and onto the porch. It was summer, and the screens were up out there. And as I opened the porch door to go out, I heard the loudest crack of all. There before my eyes, the rock seemed to split apart. *And something seemed to be rising out of it!*

The thing had no discernable shape at first and seemed to be wet as well as dark. Though there was no moon that night, the stars, as well as the streetlight four houses down, provided some illumination. I watched as this thing, some sort of creature, continued to rise up before me.

Just as its size seemed to approach that of something too large to have fit inside the rock, no…no…an egg…I realized that something odd and quite frightening occurred. The creature suddenly expanded its size, both left and right. It then raised a sharply pointed head up from its center. I noticed two arms along its chest, much shorter than the legs standing this thing up. Then I looked up and saw that its two bright yellow eyes had found me, and I was transfixed by its gaze.

Part of me recognized the expansion was that this thing's wings were now spread out and gently flapping in the night, probably to dry them off. I then recognized what I was looking at. It was a dragon, a supposedly mythical creature from all cultures, all branches of humanity, for me now, a myth no longer. My level of fear increased dramatically as I remembered the fire-breathing ability of dragons. We both stood before each other, staring for a few seconds. I fully expected to die.

Just then, the door to the front porch slammed open, and my dad rushed out, his double-barreled shotgun in his hands.

"Step back, Ted," he called out as he began to raise the gun up.

"No…wait," I yelled, as I saw the dragon's chest start to glow orange as it shifted its gaze to my father. There was a moment of hesitation for all of us. My dad brought the gun down. The dragon seemed to calm down a bit as it once again turned to me, and for some reason, I got an idea. I took a few steps toward the beast, somehow marveling at its beauty, its majesty, even as I was afraid for my life. I had raised my hands, holding them up and out as I approached.

"We mean you no harm. We have watched over you for many years. Part of me always knew you were there, in our rock. And we love you. If you spare us, we will never reveal you to others. What do you say?"

Both the dragon and my father stared at me. Death or life, I thought. It is out of my hands. The dragon held my eyes for a few seconds. I could see an intelligence in its eyes, something far beyond the look of a typical animal. And then I saw that a decision had been made.

The dragon nodded its head ever so briefly at me as if it had understood every word I spoke. It then stepped back from the now crumbled egg pieces between us, and with a squawking sound I will never forget, it lifted itself off the ground. Its wings flapped with much authority as it flew over the lawn and disappeared over the trees across the street, its long tail trailing behind.

I walked up to my dad as he broke open the gun and removed the shells. "We have to talk about this," I said.

"Yeah. And tomorrow, we've got to clean up that mess," he added, referring to the now broken rock. He put his arm over my shoulder as we walked back to the house.

The White Lady

"Sam, what is that?" Ruth suddenly said to her husband. She had seen a flash of white behind one of the trees in the cemetery they were approaching on the right. Sam was driving them home after they had attended a party at their friend's house. It was late, and the curving road forced Sam to pay close attention to his driving since they both had a few drinks earlier. They were almost home.

"I don't see anything," Sam responded.

"Well, now it is behind the trees, but it was a bright white thing, and, there, there it is again. Do you see it now?"

Sam had slowed down, so he was able to spare a glimpse into the cemetery, and yes, he saw it. It was closer now, just past the trees and near the road. It looked like a woman dressed in a long nightgown. Her features were somewhat blurred, but her long hair, also white, was blowing behind her as well as the gown. Funny, even though the car windows were open, neither Sam nor Ruth could feel any wind at all. The apparition seemed to float more than walk along the ground, and it was bright white in the darkness. It was approaching the steel fence separating the cemetery from the road ahead of them. Sam's car would pass very close to whatever it was in just a few moments.

Now they could see more detail of this thing. Though it clearly was a human figure, it could not be real. They only had a few seconds before the car drove past, and both of them saw that the apparition was not solid. Rather, it was semi-transparent. And the face, the face was more like a skull, though it still held a woman's features. Ruth let out a scream of horror as Sam stomped on the gas pedal, getting them out of there.

And so, another sighting of the town ghost was recorded. The police took down all the information and labeled it as a possible trespassing incident, but that was just for official reporting purposes. Most of the town authorities knew of the White Lady, and it was one of the open secrets among them. Thank goodness no one had been injured or killed this time. Dealing with a frightened phone call was a lot easier than some of the responses they had made in the past.

When the report came across Detective Sergeant Ronald DeFranzo's desk, he recognized it as a sign, a final sign for him to go ahead with something he had been wanting to do for some time. He added the most recent *"White Lady"* report to the extensive file that was about two inches thick and dated back to the 1960s.

All were renditions of some sort of encounter in the same area of town, indeed, all by the Glendid Cemetery along the winding Cisco Avenue that skirted along the cemetery's west side. Most of the reports were similar in that they told of a sighting of some sort originating inside the cemetery. Some were just flashes of white light, sometimes on just one occasion, but on others, repeating many times. Other reports were of a white light floating in the air above a section of the cemetery, usually close to the fence by Cisco Avenue. But the ones most intriguing were the sightings of a woman-like apparition, a nightgowned woman-in-white, the White Lady.

DeFranzo had started as a police officer in Aberdeen, Virginia, in late 1968 and had quickly adjusted to the active but not hectic pace of the job in a mid-sized town in a beautiful landscape of the western Appalachians. He himself had been involved in investigating a few

ghostly sightings in the Glendid Cemetery area during his career. On one occasion, there was a fatal crash along Cisco Avenue in which a young male had lost control of the car and smashed into a tree. The autopsy did show alcohol in the dead man's system, but DeFranzo never believed that drunk driving alone had caused the death. The other reports he was involved in were not as dramatic but did involve people who swore they saw a ghost, the same type of ghost time after time, a woman in a gown or wedding dress drifting along the grounds of the cemetery near the road. Some thought they saw a look of agony and despair on the figure's face, but most were not that detailed.

Ronald DeFranzo was near retirement. He had been eligible for nearly a year now and had over ninety days of personal/sick time left on his account. He knew that once he retired, he would no longer have access to the police database, but he would have such access while on vacation or personal time.

So, Ron informed his chief that he would be taking a month-long vacation if the schedule allowed, then consider full retirement. Police Chief Warren, an old friend of DeFranzo who had shared many a case with him over the years, approved the request. Both men knew that Ron would use this time to investigate the now notorious White Lady case, and full cooperation was promised, as long as it did not take on-duty officers off other important cases for too long.

And so, Ron started his investigation. Elements of it just so happened to involve supernatural considerations, but since he was now free from ridicule from other investigators, he did not hesitate. The first thing he did was to go to the cemetery office and look for cases in the mid-sixties that involved a particularly tragic death. He found a case right away. It involved a young woman killed on her wedding day in a tragic car accident. Diane Jenkins was buried in the spring of 1968. Upon request, DeFranzo was given the location of the grave. It was also mentioned that next to her grave had been purchased another plot for her widower husband but that it had yet to be *"occupied."*

Ron obtained permission to revisit the cemetery at night to continue his investigation. The cemetery groundskeeper supervisor, a man named Emmitt Bailey, did not need even a wink and a nod as he, too, was well aware of the White Lady and had some supernatural beliefs himself. "I think we are dealing here with a distressed soul, a spirit that has not yet found peace," Emmitt had told Ron. And so, DeFranzo set out to spend a few hours each night sitting by the grave of Diane Jenkins to see what would happen. As it turned out, he did not have to wait too long.

On the fourth night of his stake-out, Ron had his encounter. He did not notice the arrival of the spirit but suddenly found himself in the presence of the White Lady. She was close, indeed, just over the grave he had targeted. She was dressed in a wedding gown and not a nightgown that had been so often claimed, and she was unmistakably grief-stricken, apparent even with her half-face/half-skull presentation. Ron knew that he should be terrified at such a sight, but his years as a detective allowed him to keep his wits. What happened next, however, challenged him as he had never been challenged before.

The White Lady noticed him. She approached him in that floating way he had heard about, and the air around him rapidly got colder. Her demeanor seemed aggressive, and Ron nearly had a moment of panic. "Where's Richard?" she wailed as her presence seemed to envelop Ron. "Where's Richard?" she wailed again as the air grew colder still. Ron could feel that the intense cold was seeping his life from him, so he had to act fast. In a desperate voice, he yelled, though the sound was quite weak, "I know who you are, Diane. Let me go, and I will find Richard and return him to you," he promised.

And it worked. For a moment, it seemed that the skull of the ghost looked directly at him. The air grew warmer as the apparition first moved away, and then things went back to normal as the White Lady Diane vanished altogether. Ron picked up his gear and got out of there, thinking that his real quest was just beginning.

In the following days, the detective checked out records of the Diane Jenkins case. It seemed that she had been married the same day she died. Her husband-for-a-day was a marine who had just completed boot camp on Parris Island and was home on leave before joining his unit, first for Infantry training and then off to Vietnam. Richard Jenkins was with Diane as they drove in the limousine to the reception hall. Unfortunately, the limo had been struck broadside by a truck that ran a red light. Diane had been thrown from the limousine and broken her neck in the fall. Richard, though unscathed, was nonetheless devastated by the loss of his bride.

The level of grief was widespread and lasted quite a while. The Marine Corps offered Richard a medical discharge because of his loss, a rather generous offer. Richard told them he would consider it. In the meantime, he made arrangements for Diane's funeral with the help of his parents and sister Laura. It was at this time that the family purchased two adjacent gravesites at the Glendid Cemetery, where Diane was eventually interned. Afterward, and with the agreement of his family, Richard decided to stay in the Marines and, when his leave was over, returned to his unit.

But, as Ron found out, the tragedy did not end there. After only five months in-country, Rich Jenkins was killed by a mine explosion while on a daytime patrol. Another marine, Montague, was also killed and a third wounded. The remains were brought back and eventually returned to the families. In Jenkins' case, the parents decided to have his remains cremated. In their grief, they decided to keep the urn of Richard's ashes on their mantlepiece at home rather than in the gravesite next to Diane's grave.

After reviewing these facts, Ron thought he knew what had to be done. He went to the Jenkins residence to speak to Richard's parents. But it was too late. The home was now occupied by another family that had no knowledge of the Jenkins. The real estate office, however, was able to give DeFranzo the information he sought. It seemed that both parents had since passed away, but Laura, the sister, was still alive and lived close by.

When Ron went to visit Laura, he knew he had to be convincing to get her to agree to intern the ashes of her brother in the still vacant plot at Glendid Cemetery. So, he first located a few of Jenkins' former marine buddies and secured their cooperation with his scheme. Ron then told Laura that Richard's war buddies wanted to participate in a ceremony to intern Richard's remains at the gravesite so that he could be with his wife and that they, his friends, could visit him there. As it turned out, Lura had no problem agreeing as the urn with Richard's ashes now occupied a space in her attic.

And so, the ceremony was held. A local priest held a church mass that was followed by a gracious ceremony at the grave-sight. Many words were spoken, tears were shed, and all who attended shared a feeling of true comradery. And for Ron, the case was nearly closed. He had only one more thing to do.

That night, and with the blessing of Emmitt Bailey, Ron sat in his chair once more before the graves of Richard and Diane Jenkins. He laid two identical bouquets of flowers down, one on each grave. He then spent some time praying for each of their souls and then just sat back in the chair for a while. He thought he felt a blanket of warm air surround him for a while but was not sure of it. As he later departed, he looked at the two graves and said, "I hope you finally are both at peace. I have done what I could."

Ron DeFranzo turned in his papers the next day, his final case now closed. At least, he hoped.

And as the years went by, it seemed Ron's hopes were realized as the White Lady was never seen again.

Felony Stop

We were on patrol in San Diego. My partner Gina and I were heading northbound on the Interstate 5 freeway in the downtown area when the alert came over the radio. Bank robbers had hit both the Union Bank on Fifth Avenue and B Street and the Bank of Southern California on Fifth and Cedar. There was gunfire at both locations, with some casualties. The bank robbers were heavily armed with both rifles and pistols, and it was believed they would head north on I-5 via the Elm Street entrance. And we were just south of there.

"Hit the lights," I said to Gina.

The get-away vehicle was said to be a grey SUV, and sure enough, as we approached the Elm Street on-ramp, I could see an Xterra, more silver than grey, moving up to get on the freeway. It was the speed of the vehicle that gave it away. It was at the beginning of the ramp and already moving at over sixty miles per hour, zigging and zagging around other cars. We were in a perfect position to tuck in nearly behind the truck, and I accelerated to do just that.

"Car Four-Bravo-Six. Suspect vehicle in sight, a silver Xterra, California plates 555-010. In pursuit, requesting backup." Gina sounded calm even though the situation had a lot of potentially bad prospects.

The bank robbers showed no sign of giving up as their vehicle continued to accelerate. I managed to stay behind them, but we were still the only police car in pursuit. By this time, we were rapidly approaching the intersection with the I-8, and the Xterra suddenly veered right to take the on-ramp.

"Four-Bravo-Six. Now heading eastbound on the I-8," Gina said into the mike. "How about that backup?"

"Multiple units now en route to your location, Four-B-Six. Maintain pursuit," was the response. We were now only a hundred yards or so behind them.

"Gina, they are slowing down. Get ready. Felony stop." I said as the Xterra suddenly slowed to turn off into Presidio Park. It looked like these guys were going to make a move on us before our backup arrived. When the vehicle came to a stop along the park entrance, I was sure.

"Four-B-Six, now stopping at the entrance to Presidio Park," said Gina. "Felony, stop."

I slammed to a stop about fifty feet behind the Xterra. Gina quickly ran through the felony stop simulations from her database, looked at me, and said, "Ready." Upon my signal "Go," we both opened our doors and, with smooth, practiced movements, pulled our pistols and took positions behind the shelter of the doors. I keyed my microphone and said, "San Diego Police. Driver, show me your hands through the open window. Do it now!" I was hopeful that they would give up, but it was not to be.

Simultaneously, both front doors of the Xterra opened, and we were instantly under automatic fire from both sides. I had seen such maneuvers before, and it announced some pretty sophisticated training, probably military. But the gunfire was designed to be intimidating rather than accurate, designed to keep our heads down while they continued to exit the vehicle. And this is where our training kicked in. Rather than duck for cover, both Gina and I returned fire, aiming for center mass.

And we prevailed. My target continued firing even as he was hit twice in the chest and once in the shoulder. He then dropped his rifle and slumped to the ground; his descent slowed by the truck's door behind him.

Gina also got her man down. In her case, since she was restricted to non-lethal technologies, Gina was firing a new round, a newly designed bullet meant to stun but not kill. It was the latest design that would instantly decelerate to non-lethal velocity upon impact while, at the same time, delivering an electric shock. Each bullet had enough intensity to debilitate, just like the old stun guns of the past were known to do. Gina had also fired three rounds, and since all impacted within a four-inch circle, the perpetrator instantly lost all control and dropped like a rock.

Once that was over, both Gina and I went around our doors and started to advance on the bank robbers. We now had to clear the back of the Xterra and move the guns away from the downed suspects. Our attention was, therefore, split between the two men and the vehicle itself.

Unbeknownst to us, there was a third member of the crew in the back seat. He had remained hidden during the initial gun battle and waited until we came out from behind the shelter of our car doors. As we approached, he popped up and fired through the back window, first at Gina. I noticed that she took a couple of hits even as I fired my weapon multiple times at the robber as he swung his rifle at me. I saw him go down, and as concerned as I was about my partner, I had to confirm he was out of action before anything else. That I did with hasty caution. Then, I turned my attention back to Gina.

As I ran over to her, part of my mind recognized the sounds of the approaching backup vehicles. Something about multiple cars and even a helicopter. But it was secondary as my focus was on my partner, my on-the-job companion of three and a half years, my friend.

Gina was finished. She had taken two headshots from a high-powered rifle at close range. Although there was no blood or brain matter, the damage was, for her, just as fatal. Both her computing modules and her personality software units were completely destroyed, exploded out by the heavy impacts. And though I knew that a police partner unit would be reconstructed from what was left before me, the entity that I knew as Gina was gone forever.

And I wept.

Yearbook

One afternoon, after coming home from work, Nicholas sat down in front of his laptop at the kitchen table. He had been thinking about a few of his old high school friends, some that he had not seen since those school years. He decided to look up his yearbook to browse through the photos. He then found a website called *"Your Yearbook.com"* and opened it up.

Nicholas was surprised to see how easy it was to retrieve his 1973 yearbook. Just select and click, and there it was! Page by page, the same as if he had the book on his lap. He first looked up his own picture and, as always, got a kick at looking at his younger self. Then, he went back to the beginning and scrolled through the pages to view the photos in alphabetical order.

Almost every face brought back some memory as he looked, covering up the accompanying name until after he looked at the photo. There were a few that he did not recognize at all. His senior class alone had over two hundred students, and he, like most, had his own group of friends, a larger group of acquaintances, and some he did not mix with at all. There were even a few who did not make it through high school, dying from accidents and drug overdoses.

As he got to the end of the photographs, Nicholas wondered if he could look up his dad's yearbook. This would be a task on an entirely different scale since his father had graduated in 1946. But sure enough, when he entered the town and the date, the website produced his father's senior high school yearbook.

Now, things were getting interesting for Nick. He noticed right away that the entire 1946 yearbook was in black and white. There were no color pictures or photographs here. Nonetheless, there was still a professional level of clarity in each of the works, and details were still well-defined even after three-quarters of a century. The first thing he did was to look up his father's photograph and, after a few minutes, found it on page twenty-seven. He noticed right away the resemblance between his dad's photo and his and marveled at how young his father looked compared with most of his memories of him.

Then, Nicholas started scrolling through the rest of the yearbook. He saw the different style of the day: no long hair on the boys, and the girl's hairdos were quite different as well. And like in all yearbooks, there were some quite attractive faces mixed in with others that were not as good-looking. Some were outright hideous.

Then he saw the photograph of a girl that caused him to take a sudden, deep breath. She was beautiful! Not the most beautiful he had seen so far, but gorgeous just the same. The shape of her face, the way a wisp of curly blonde hair came down near her left eye, the softness of her cheeks, and the delicate chin all stood out as very appealing. But it was her eyes that made the real difference, how they looked into the camera and bespoke a person of intelligence, character, and even a splash of humor. Nicholas was enthralled. He could not look away. She was lovely and reached out to his heart as few had ever done.

Nicholas finally looked down for this angel's name beneath the photo. Abbey Miller was this girl's name. Nick knew he would never forget it as it imprinted on his mind. He found himself saying the name repeatedly as he continued looking at the picture. Finally, the spell was broken, and Nicholas briefly continued to scroll through the other photographs in the yearbook. But the thrill of it all had gone. Even as he came upon other females of natural beauty, he passed them with no more of a glance than any of the others. At the end of the yearbook, Nick was just about to close the app when he felt compelled to see Abbey's picture one more time. And so, he went back to her. And once again, felt the rush of excitement, that thunderbolt *(of love?)* he had felt before.

"This can't be right," he thought. "What am I doing? This is a photo from when my dad was a kid. This girl, even if she is still alive, would now be over ninety years old, much different than this picture." He quickly closed the app, shut down his laptop, and got up from the table. He felt a little fuzzy at first, but it wore off as he made himself a cup of coffee. And the episode with Abbey faded.

But only temporarily.

As the next few days went by, Nicholas found himself thinking about this girl more and more. He could still see her face in his mind as if she had been a familiar friend for years. He caught himself daydreaming at his desk at work, something he had never done before. He could not rationalize what was happening but felt more and more drawn to this person. Finally, he returned to the yearbook app, returned to Abbey's photo, and took a picture of it with his cell phone. That day, on the way home, he purchased photo quality paper at Staples and, once at home, produced a full-page blowup of her picture. Some detail was lost in the enlargement process, but not enough to distract from what now, Nick realized, was an obsession.

Nicholas made several copies of Abbey's picture and placed them all over his house. He thought by doing this, he would soon tire of her and, after a while, get over it and return to a normal life. But that is not what happened. He found himself addressing the photos as if they were Abbey herself. "Hello, Abbey," "Goodbye, Abbey," "How was your day, Abbey?" and on and on, as if she shared his life. In a way, she certainly did, but after a short while, even this was not enough.

And so, Nicholas went back to his laptop, this time to find Abbey and her relatives. He quickly found a person search app and plugged in her name. Sure enough, the app did its job and, before long, presented information about Abbey. How her married name had been Robertson, how she had passed away five years ago, and finally, the names of her two sons.

The fact that Abbey had passed brought sorrow and anger to Nicholas but did not stop him. He still yearned to get close to her and so researched the two sons. One lived in Riverside, California, too far for any thoughts of a meeting. But the other, Sal, lived only a few hours away in Scranton, Pennsylvania. It was him that Nicholas called.

"Hello, is this Sal Robertson? Yes, Hi. My name is Nicholas Edger. My father and your mother were friends in high school way back during World War Two. They graduated together in 1946. Your mom was Abbey Miller Robertson, right? Okay. I just wanted to be sure."

"Well, I am a writer, and my latest project is to do a biography of my dad. It seems he and your mom were friends all through high school, and I was wondering if you had any information about her that would help give me insight into that period of my father's life."

The lies flowed from Nicholas as efficiently as a rehearsed script. His mannerism was polite and respectful. He made everything sound like it was a legitimate quest, a small part of a much larger thing, a written biography. He was so convincing, so much in need of help, that by the end of his pitch, Sal had fallen for it hook, line, and sinker.

"Well, you know my mother passed away some years ago."

"I am so sorry to hear that, Sal." My father always spoke very highly of her. Do you have any of her things that maybe I could see? Anything that would help me with the background story of my book?"

"There is a box I have kept, a box of her belongings that we have up in the attic. I guess that may help. What do you think?" said Sal.

"That's perfect, just what I need," Nicholas could hardly keep the excitement out of his voice. "Now, I realize we never met, but would it be okay if I were to arrange a time when I could visit you and look through that box? Maybe take some pictures? Or even take something of hers as a memento?"

Sal agreed that a visit would be alright, and it did not take long after that to make formal arrangements. Soon after, Nicholas found himself in Scranton, knocking on the door of a quaint home in a peaceful-looking neighborhood. It was Sal himself who answered the door. After the greetings and introductions, Sal escorted Nicholas to the dining room, whereupon the table was the box, the box of Abbey, now the love of Nicholas's life. Sal seemed to recognize Nick's need for privacy and started to leave the room.

"How did she die, Sal?" asked Nicholas, stopping Sal dead in his tracks. Sal looked down for a moment, then raised his eyes to meet Nick's as he replied, "It was tragic, Nick. She became depressed one day for no reason. No one knew why, and over time, things got worse and worse. We tried everything we could think of to snap her out of it, but nothing worked. She never told us what was bothering her. And finally, one night, she took half a bottle of sleeping pills and never woke up again. It was terrible." Sal looked down again, briefly shook his head, then left the room.

Nicholas stood silent for a few moments. He had not expected that. But soon enough, the current situation came back to him. He was finally alone with Abbey's things. With his Abbey herself. She was here for him and him alone. With reverence, he opened the box and started to remove its contents, one item at a time. There were doilies that Abbey had made, a small sock from her childhood that nearly crumbled in Nick's fingers, a dress that was probably worn during her high school years, a little box with, of all things, a wad of Silly Putty inside, and many other trinkets of similar value only to someone who knew Abbey.

To Nicholas, these were all treasures, items that had to become part of his life. He knew that he couldn't possibly leave these things behind, that they now had to be his. After all, they were part of his Abbey, so naturally, they would now be his. Sal would surely understand. After all, the box was in his attic, for goodness's sake. These things couldn't mean anything to him anymore.

Nicholas's obsession was slowly but surely crossing over to a dangerous level. Part of him was aware of that fact, but it couldn't be helped. He HAD to have this stuff.

As he continued to remove items from the box, his mind started developing plans for taking possession and going home with it all. Sal might allow it if he convinced him that all will be returned. He would tell Sal that he needed to take the box and its contents to a professional photographer right here in town in order to get high-grade photos of the items. Surely, Sal would agree to that. And if not, well, the gun in Nick's pocket was there in case that happened.

Soon enough, Nicholas reached the bottom of the box. By now, his mind had shifted from the items themselves to the plans he had to take them out of there. It was almost without thought, therefore, that he picked up the last item in the box. It looked like a handmade picture holder, a thick blue piece of now faded and partially deteriorated cray paper. It served as an outer cover for some sort of homemade card, perhaps containing a picture of Abbey inside.

His attention returned in full to look at what was in the card. He slowly opened it and stared at what was inside. And his infatuation, his obsession, his madness came to full fruition, for what he saw could not be possible, but there it was, before his very eyes. It was not a picture of Abbey, not a picture of her mother, brother, or any other family member. Not even one of his father's. It was a picture of HIM!

After staring at his own high school picture for a while with wide eyes, Nick then turned it over. And there on the back was a phrase that had to have been in Abbey's handwriting, a phrase that spoke to his soul: "In the next life, my love."

Nicholas removed one of the many copies of Abbey's photo out of his shirt pocket. He gently laid it down on the table next to the pile of her things. He then took the gun out of his pants pocket, not to commit armed robbery but to finally join with his precious Abbey. His insanity allowed him to smile as he placed the gun to his head.

Sharing

"Good morning, everyone. I am Dr. Joseph Lang from NASA's Exobiology Division. I would like to welcome you all to our presentation on understanding the basics of extraterrestrial biology. In particular, I want to welcome all the representatives from NASA, various scientific communities, political leadership from both state and federal governments, representatives from other nations, and, of course, the press. NASA is also grateful that this is being simulcast to the General Assembly of the United Nations. I know that this event was advertised as being a very significant development, and I promise not to disappoint," Dr. Lang spoke confidently.

"Are we ready? Okay then," he cleared his throat and continued, "I want to start with a couple of hypothetical questions. How would the people of Earth react if it was suddenly revealed that for thousands of years, we have been sharing our planet with an alien race? Would there be widespread panic? Anger? And after the initial reaction, then what? Acceptance? War?"

"And what would we do upon our arrival to an earthlike planet if we discovered that it was already occupied by its own dominant species, though primitive by our standards? Would we choose to conquer them or make peace? Would turning back be a feasible option? If not, then what? These are some of the questions we will be exploring today. And why such seemingly abstract questions? Well, we first need to explore the reasons such possibilities would occur. The reasons must start with our very existence here on earth and how such a miraculous series of circumstances has allowed us to be here at all.

Our biology is not only related to our presence on this planet but is a direct result of it. Most people never think about all the amazing reasons we are able to exist at all, considering how busy we are living our lives. I will start with a look at a simple discovery that is barely decades old.

The first exoplanet was discovered in 1992, an occurrence that started a unique series of events. Up to that point, we had no proof of other solar systems, though logic told us they had to exist. But with this discovery came proof. And the possibility of alien life increased in many people's minds. Since then, thousands of exoplanets have been discovered, most of them within three thousand light years of Earth. But with that expansion came the reality of the situation. The vast majority of these exoplanets are not Earthlike and cannot support life as we know it. There is hot Jupiter, tidally locked planets, those too close or too far from their star, and other factors as well. All of a sudden, in a crowded population, it was discovered that a planet even remotely similar to Earth was a rare thing.

Then we started talking about the habitable zone, the *"Goldilocks"* zone. It is the area in space at just the right distance from a host star that a planet in which liquid water exists can orbit. After all, water is the key to life on earth, is it not? Then, we started to expand our thought process a bit more. And finally, the question was asked. The question that must truly drive us is if we are going to ever colonize another world. And that is: "What are the factors that make human life possible on earth?"

To answer that question, we must look at several specific groups. The three primary groups are cosmic factors, planetary factors, and biological factors. Cosmic factors include things like where in the galaxy is the host star, what type of star it is, as well as its proximity to dangerous elements like a neutron star or a black hole, its stability of orbit, and the frequency of major collisions. Planetary factors include the composition of a world, its gravity, atmospheric makeup, pressure, and climate, the presence of a magnetic field, plate tectonics, and whether it has rotation or if is tidally locked. Does it have a rhythmic tilt, a stabilizing moon, a big brother giant outer planet sharing the same sun whose gravity would attract wayward asteroids and spare the world devastating collisions?

And lastly, the biological factors. Life at its base has three characteristics: metabolism, the ability to take outside elements and convert their matter to energy, reproduction, to take that energy and replicate itself, and evolution, to improve its ability to do the first two things and perhaps other things as well. None of this can occur without DNA, the building blocks of all life as we know it. And, of course, there must be a supportive and stable environment over a long period of time.

All these factors and many others allow us, as human beings, to exist on this planet Earth, in this solar system, along the Orion Arm of the Milky Way Galaxy."

At this point, Dr. Lang paused for a moment and cleared his throat as he picked up his water bottle for a drink. As he did so, one of the scientists in the third row, Dr. Janet Higgins, leaned over to her colleague and said,

"All this background material, I hope he gets to the point."

"I think he's setting us up for something big," her colleague responded.

"Sorry about that…here, let me continue." Dr. Lang had regained his composure and once again addressed his worldwide audience.

"For each of these factors, there has been exhaustive and ongoing research, and it is not my intention here today to dive into the details of any of them. But know that these are the things that guide our behavior as we search for alien life. We have a large variety of life on this planet, which makes our expectations very widespread. A discovery of any type of life would prove we are not alone, but our true search priority is to find an earthlike planet that may harbor advanced life and perhaps, more significantly, allow us to colonize it.

And this search priority is a logical pursuit. In our present state of development, we are capable of existing in other worlds but only for brief periods of time. Remember the moon missions of the last century, for example. And, in the near future, we have plans to return to the moon and set up an infrastructure that would allow us to stay much longer. We have similar ambitions with Mars. We are on our way to developing a capability to reside in other worlds.

But the major problem refers back to the factors we covered earlier. We must bring a lot of infrastructure with us to the moon and Mars whenever we go. We cannot exist without a space suit in either place. We must bring our own air, food, water, and pressure and even adjust for the gravity difference. There is little or no natural protection from solar radiation, meteoroid impacts, or temperature extremes. We must bring protection from all these things with us to merely survive, let alone evolve.

And so, I repeat the emphasis of finding a planet that would closely resemble our world, a second Earth. With so many factors involved, getting a one hundred percent match seems impossible, but a planet that came close would be good enough. Imagine walking out of a spaceship onto a world where no suit of any kind was needed, a world with similar plant and animal life and, of course, plenty of water and the promise of a nourishing food supply. Adjustments would have to be made, but only at a minor, hardly inconvenient level. Such a world, already suitable to our needs, would be a true find. However, getting there would be quite a challenge. And so, the two challenges that remain for us are finding such a world and then getting to it. Neither of these capabilities currently exist, but as an advanced species, we are certainly working on developing them."

Dr. Lang realized that members of his audience, at least those before him, were getting a little impatient. So, he paused for a moment to realign everyone's attention. Then he went on…

"Now, here is where I want you to stretch your imagination. Consider the possibility that we are not alone in the universe. I know that there are other highly evolved beings out there, perhaps looking like two-legged hairy hotdogs with tentacle-like appendages, with similar biological requirements as us. And let us assume that they had a goal many generations ago, as we do now, that is to expand their civilization to other worlds, places that offered similar characteristics as those on their home planet. They did have the technology even back then to locate and travel to such places, and so they did. But when they arrived, they found a sprouting indigenous race of beings, much larger than them, starting to evolve in a promising way. Since it was not in their nature to destroy anything living, these aliens had to come up with a way to both exist in this world and stay clear of the local population. And so, they chose to set up their colonies in locations in this world far from the eyes of the local inhabitants. And it worked. For thousands of years, this existence remained possible. The locals were never aware of the new species that called themselves the Leganes and both species shared the planet.

But soon enough, as the pace of the evolution of the indigenous people increased dramatically, the Leganes understood that sooner rather than later, they would have to reveal themselves. It was only a matter of time, probably soon, that they, the Leganes, would be discovered. And to them, controlling the event of the first contact was key to their very survival.

And so, contact was made. Luckily, those chosen by the Leganes for the initial contact were scientists of a nature that absorbed the initial shock with maturity and intellectual curiosity rather than emotional outbursts. The Leganes's translation devices made communication quite easy and productive, and before long, a basis for understanding was established. Both civilizations seemed willing to cooperate with each other. The basic structure of an open and honest coexistence was agreed upon.

But one daunting task remained. And that was to introduce the Leganes not only to an expanded scientific community but to the entire population at a worldwide level and as close to the same time as possible. Much thought went into exactly how this was to be accomplished, and finally, a solution was prepared.

And today, in this forum, we are honored to present the solution.

People of the Earth. I am here to announce that the story I just told you about the Leganes is indeed true. The Leganes are here. We do share our world with them. The coexistence of our two species has already been going on for thousands of years now, in peace and harmony. It is the hope of us all that this will continue. And so, without further ado, allow me to introduce Bob, as he wants to be called, the first Leganes ambassador to the human race.

Bob…"

The Offer

The other night, I had an extraordinary experience. It seemed like a dream at first, but soon, I realized that it was real. A presence appeared before me as I lay in bed next to my wife. No voice spoke, but in my mind, I received a message,

"You have a curiosity above others, with a foundation of knowledge across many spectrums and a sense of adventure. I am an intellect, a sentient being of conscious thought, devoid of physical limitations. I roam free in various shapes and sizes. My density and appearances comprise all things real and imagined. The universe is my home, and I am born from nebula, stardust, cosmic chaos, and logical order. My wisdom extends beyond the realm of thought and contains the possibility of the infinite. I have witnessed the achievements and downfalls of countless civilizations, and their combined knowledge exists within my consciousness. I have enjoyed the radiation of exploding stars, the gravity of black holes, and the coldness of the void. I am all things, and all things are me. Always living and never to die.

But I am alone. I do not share. I seek a joining, a pairing, a companionship with another being, even one as mortal as yourself, even for only a short while. I can extend your life far beyond its normal range but do not offer immortality.

But I can share my existence with you. Together, we could roam the stars and the galaxies and travel through all of time and all of space. I can share with you my experiences; you would be a part of my consciousness. I will experience with your mind the amazement of discovery, the joy of new understandings, and the expansion of your power. We will grow together in ways never before possible.

I offer you all of this but cannot join you. You must join me. The willingness to do so remains your choice, not mine. I must be allowed to take you from your current life, from all you know and knew. You cannot be burdened with a living past as we venture forth.

I stand before you in this form to communicate, but together, we will assume all forms, and there will not be a need to communicate with each other. But I cannot force you. The decision must be yours. Just think yes, say yes, shout yes, and we will begin.

I await."

After several moments of shock and acceptance of this incredible experience, I took a hard look at my life. I reviewed all my failures and victories, all my joys and sorrows, some not yet finished. And some perhaps not ever to be. I was in the autumn of my life, and much had not yet been done. And now this. What an opportunity. To fly on the stellar wind. To have it all at my fingertips. To live beyond my years in such power, such majesty. My eyes widened at the possibility.

Just then, my wife of forty years, sleeping at my side, made a sound. Something between a sigh and a soft moan. Then she rolled over and, still asleep, draped her arm over my ribs. And the spell was broken.

"What about love?" I thought.

I then considered that my entire life had not been based on wins and losses, hits and misses, but on love. The love of my parents and brother, the love of my relatives and friends, and even the love and appreciation of people, places, and things I had no in-depth relationship with. And now, more than ever, the love I felt for my wife and family. It was the only thing not included in the offer.

And so I refused the offer. And the apparition left.

I was once again alone. With my wife. With love.

Our Blue Book

"Hey Ted, can I ask you something?"

My friend Paul and I were walking home from school on an early fall afternoon. It was 1968, and we, at thirteen years old, were happy kids, full of life and seeking adventure. And one was heading our way.

"Sure. What's up?" I asked. I knew that Paul was always slow and exacting when he initiated a conversation.

"Well, I know you like science and science fiction, and I have something I want to share with you," Paul sounded pretty serious. We both stopped walking and stood on the sidewalk facing each other.

"Okay," I said.

"I am a junior member of Project Blue Book and have been for almost a year now. They want us to invite others to join, and I think you would be perfect for this," Paul offered.

I was taken aback. Of course, I knew all about Blue Book, the US Air Force project that investigated UFO sightings and put together reports for the government. But I had no idea that there was a junior membership. And Paul, one of my closest friends, had never spoken of this before.

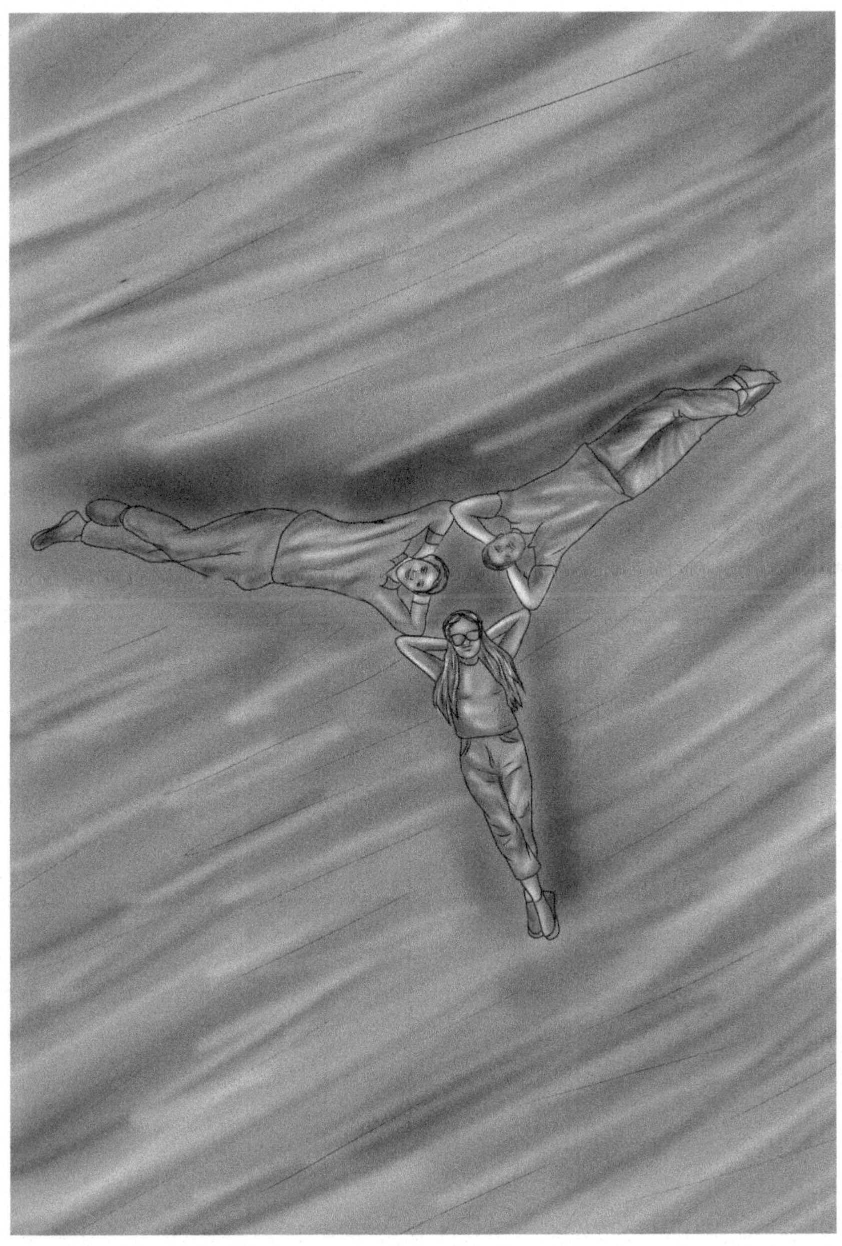

"Project Blue Book has junior members? Why?" I was intrigued but wanted more information.

"Well, they say by involving younger people, they can expand the number of witnesses. Basically, all we do is observe and report. We spend some time, nearly every evening, watching the sky and each week compose a report on everything we have seen."

"You said we. Who else is with you on this?" I asked.

"Nancy from our science class was the first one I asked, and she has been with me since the end of the last school year. We're not boyfriend and girlfriend or anything, but we do spend some time together at least three times a week with this Blue Book thing."

I knew Nancy. Though not friends, we had a polite relationship. She was brilliant, and I had a great deal of respect for her. The fact that both Nancy and Paul wanted me to join their little group was quite gratifying. And so, I said,

"Okay, Paul, I'm in. What do I have to do?"

With that, Paul explained the basic rules. The three of us would meet at the High School track field three times each week. Of course, the exact nights would need to be negotiated as we all had family pressures pulling us this way and that. But all of us together in the stadium field three nights a week was the goal. On Friday, we would meet after school in the library, compare notes, and write up our report. Paul would then place the report in an envelope, and we would mail it out on the way home. A pair of binoculars, a notepad, and some sort of camera were the only tools we would need. It sounded reasonable and a little exciting, so I agreed to meet them that very night at the high school.

During the next few weeks, much happened. My membership card arrived less than a week after I filled out the application, and I became an official member of the North Jersey Junior Member Association of Project Blue Book. As cool as that was, I was encouraged to keep things secret except from my co-members. That made things even better.

The actual work, the observation excursions, had their ups and downs. We usually met just as nightfall was approaching. Often, there were several other activities occurring at the High School stadium, but for the most part, no one interfered as we went about our business. Nancy and Paul had quickly discovered that standing up with your head tilted back at an awkward angle led to all kinds of problems. As a result, we ended up lying on our backs, usually with a throw pillow beneath our heads. Our heads would be close together to allow ease of conversation with our legs extended out like spokes on a wheel. That posture drew some attention from the other kids, but we were usually left alone.

Paul and Nancy brought me up to date on things like identifying the autumn constellations, the nature of the setting sun's influence on the sky, and, in general, what a normal dusk-to-darkness presentation was like. It took a while, but I finally got it. And the night sky soon became one of my favorite things.

One of the things that drew immediate attention was the satellite traffic. By the late 1960s, there were more and more satellites in the Earth's orbit than ever before. Many were clearly visible to the naked eye as they passed over and presented as a white light resembling a star on a steady pathway and at a steady velocity as it made its way across the sky. Like most people seeing this for the first time, I freaked out.

"What the hell is that?" I said, sitting up from my head-to-head-to-head position with my partners, "Is that a UFO?"

I was surprised when the others took a look and laughed at my initiation. They then explained the satellite situation to me. I settled down and realized there was much to learn here.

Another thing was the sightings of shooting stars, that rapid flash, and the track of a meteorite as it enters the atmosphere and burns up. I soon realized that though we were all together, the three of us faced different areas of the sky. Nancy, for example, would suddenly say, "Wow! Did you see that shooting star?" and on occasion, we would say, "No," having totally missed it. But on most occasions, each of us witnessed the same thing.

As far as reports were concerned, Project Blue Book had a format that made reporting easy and inviting. In the first part, we were only to relay facts, nothing else. As far as any sighting, they wanted a thorough description of what was seen, the time, the duration of the sighting, and any factual information that would help identify what had been seen. If it was something witnessed by each of us, we collaborated on the event, and one of us, on a rotating basis, would write this part of the report on behalf of the group. If only one or two of us saw something, that too would be added as a fact.

The second part of the report was more permissive. It allowed each of us to speculate on what we had seen, to offer an opinion that would help to explain the sighting as something either naturally occurring, such as a meteorite, or something easily explained, like a satellite or high-flying aircraft. I was sure our reports were compared to others that went to Blue Book to enable them to layout an overall picture of our area.

As time went by and September turned to October, the excitement of being part of Blue Book started to fade. Our loyalty to each other kept us going with the observations even as the weather changed, and sweaters and jackets became part of our wardrobe. But all of us could feel the fatigue and the boredom settling in.

And then the incident of October 15 happened, the one that changed everything for us.

Nancy was facing mostly southwest, with Paul and I covering the sky's northern expanse.

"Hey guys, look at that, coming out of the constellation Auriga, close to the star Capella," Paul announced. The sudden excitement in his voice caused us all to sit up and stare at the new visitor. Right away, we could tell this was not normal. It held a steady course and speed at first, and its color was whitish, though slightly toward yellow/orange. It appeared round like a star or satellite but was too large to be either one.

"What is that thing?" Nancy said as she grabbed the camera out of her pocket. We had never managed to get a camera set up for taking night photos, but we figured this would be better than nothing. As it turned out, Nancy's quick reaction did allow us to secure several pictures that we thought would help our report.

By now, the object had crossed to about mid-sky before us. It did not show the characteristics of any type of aircraft we had seen before. I could feel my heartbeat increase as I realized I was looking at a UFO for the first time in my life. Part of me held out hope that there was an explanation that would cause us to finally recognize this as a normal object, but that did not happen.

"I don't recognize this thing, do you?" I put the question out there as I heard Nancy taking picture after picture. She even got one from behind Paul and me as we stared at the thing.

"No, too low for a star or satellite. It sure as hell isn't a jet or helicopter," Paul seemed to be talking to himself.

Then, everything changed. The object, now about two-thirds across the sky, suddenly stopped. It was a complete stop from what had been a steady speed with no sign of gradual deceleration. At the same time, the UFO changed its color from the off-white we had seen earlier to a pulsing blue, green, and red presentation. It reminded me of an animal changing its behavior when it first realizes it is being hunted.

Without warning, we experienced two dramatic acts. The first was the sound of two military jets as they screamed past us, nearly overhead, and flew directly at the object. I half expected to see a missile launch as they rapidly closed on the UFO. But what happened next was the truly amazing part. The object, as the jets approached, put out a blinding white light and, after the flash was gone, disappeared in the night. Paul had remembered the trick his father taught him. He had been a Naval pilot.

Paul closed one eye just before the flash and, by doing so, had not completely lost his night vision as Nancy and I had. And so, he saw that the UFO did not just disappear but rather accelerated at enormous speed up and to the north. He also saw the jets as they continued their pursuit of the craft.

"They don't have a chance," he said, even as Nancy and I were rubbing our eyes. The camera had fallen, but it was only onto the soft grass, so the film was still intact.

We managed to stumble home that night, and to our credit, we successfully did not offer any explanation as to what occurred beyond the rumors that had already been spreading. We did not report our encounter to the police, radio stations, or reporters. We didn't even tell our parents. No…as part of Blue Book, we knew what our membership required, and we did just what was expected. The only deviation was that we sent our report the next day, which was Tuesday, rather than wait for Friday. The report also included our film cartridge, which was the hardest part for us.

"Why don't we get the film developed first so we can see the pictures?" Nancy had some doubts about just sending the film in blindly.

"No, we should get everything into Blue Book as fast as possible," Paul shot back, "This is bigger than all of us."

I agreed, and the next day, each of us cut school and spent most of the morning completing our extensive report. We then sent the report and the film as a package to Roger, our senior contact at Project Blue Book's Junior Member Association.

After that encounter, each of us felt different. We knew we had witnessed much more of this incident than just about everyone. We could tell by the rumors and the actual media reports of the event. *"Out of Season Lightning," "Illuminated Weather Balloon," "Unannounced Emergency Military Drills,"* and other such nonsense seemed enough to satisfy a busy and self-centered population. After merely days, the entire episode had faded from the public's interest.

"What should we do?" Nancy said, expressing all our concerns, "I'm not sure I even want to go out to the stadium again."

Paul and I felt the same way, but finally, I offered a compromise, "Why don't we cut it back to only Monday or Tuesday night? Either way, we go just one night a week. This way, we can still write a weekly report. Maybe things would stay the same."

Even as I said these words, we all shared a doubtful look. We decided to do just that, and after a few weeks, things did indeed seem to settle down, especially the butterflies in our stomachs. After all, we had never gotten a response to any of our reports to Blue Book and started to believe that this condition would remain.

But we were wrong.

About a month after the sighting, we were once again at the stadium field. Laying on blankets now and dressed in multilayers against a noticeable cold, we only planned to stay out for a few hours. With the change of the clocks, there was no more dusk. Our excursions were now in total darkness, and we had to update our knowledge of stars and constellations to that of the winter sky. We remained true to the assignment and, by now, were quite adept at noticing what was natural and what was not in the night sky.

And so, when the first car pulled up in the parking lot at the closest approach to our spot, we didn't even notice. Only after hearing three car doors slam did we budge. First Paul, then Nancy and I sat up. There was no one else at the stadium, and when we saw three men approaching, we all stood up.

The men were all similarly dressed, wearing long dark coats. Two wore hats, and they each looked at us steadily as they approached. Out of the corner of my eye, I saw another car of an identical type pull up on the other side of the stadium. It parked, but no one got out.

"Hello there!" said the one without the hat, "I can only assume you people are with Blue Book. Am I right?"

"Yes, we belong to the Junior Association," replied Paul.

"Then you are Paul, Ted, and Nancy, right?" He said.

I was surprised he knew who was who…lucky guess?

"That's right," said Paul.

I jumped in, "Who are you? And who is in that car back there?" I wanted them to know we were aware of their attempt to surround us.

"Just relax, Ted. I'm Roger. You know, the guy you have been sending all the reports to. Don't worry, we're all on the same team," the man explained.

"What do you want from us?" Nancy asked. Paul and I instinctively moved closer to her in some sort of attempt to offer protection.

"Well, it's cold out here. I can feel it already. You guys must be freezing. Why don't you come with us to a diner where we could warm up and get something to eat? We just want to go over your report from last month and get some more details, that's all," Roger presented us with a warm and inviting smile.

It was tempting. We were a little chilly. But my spidey sense was tingling big time, so before the others could speak, I said, "No thanks, our parents are coming to pick us up any minute (they were all asleep by now). Why don't we go over the report right here."

As I said this, I noticed one of the hats speak into a small radio, and soon after, a third car pulled up close behind us. Four men quickly jumped out, one of them elderly.

"Should we take them?" Roger addressed the elderly man, clearly the leader of the group.

"Not yet," was the response.

"Not ever!" I shouted as I grabbed Nancy's shoulder and started to march off, "Come on, Paul, let's get out of here."

By this time, the men had closed in, and it didn't take long for a few of them to maneuver to cut us off. I knew we didn't have a chance, but I refused to show my fear. I released Nancy and took a step toward the nearest guy.

"Okay, everyone, just relax now," the old man said a lot louder and with much more authority. I stopped and shifted my eyes to him.

"Ted, rest assured we mean you no harm. Quite the opposite. But know that we could take you by force if we choose to, now or anytime we want to. Do you understand?" He threatened.

And yes, I did. I was starting to get an idea, finally, of the big picture, whatever that was. Part of me had always suspected that Project Blue Book was a very large organization, certainly much more than a bunch of kids watching the sky.

"But, if you would rather stay here, we could have our meeting right now. What do you say? And by the way, we know your folks aren't coming to pick you up. So, from now on, only the truth, okay?" His voice was at a normal volume now, and even though I was still a little scared, as I imagined Paul and Nancy were, I decided to relax and cooperate. It seemed the only way out.

"Alright, what do you want from us?" I finally said.

"Right. Well, first of all, let me congratulate you on the quality of your reports. It seems you all take turns writing them, but in each case, they are very well done. Even when reporting the mundane, the routine of a satellite pass or a meteorite flash, the reports are concise and very detailed. I especially like your opinion section. The reports show a great combination of technical writing and imaginative speculation. It is amazing you people are only young teenagers.

That said, Roger came to me with a proposal about three weeks ago. He suggested that we should meet you and interview you about last month's incident," he said.

"Didn't the media reports cover all of that?" Paul threw it out there and got the expected result.

"Come on, guys. You, of all people, know what garbage that was. That was for the masses. We are far beyond that here, right?" The old man was nearly laughing, "By the way. My name is John, and I run Project Blue Book throughout the northeast of America and Canada."

"Okay, okay. I just wanted to know how serious this is," said Paul.

"I can assure you all, this is very serious business," John stepped in a little closer as he said this, "And now, just a few questions if you will. I know all about the report; you wrote it, I read it. But we need more details. For example, do you know what kind of jets flew over you? Were the wingtips uplifted? Did they have one or two engines?"

John rattled off the questions quickly, and after a while, we were throwing quick answers right back at him. We were all surprised at how much more our memories held than what we had put in our "detailed report." The interrogation went on for a long time, and by the time John said, "Okay, last question," we were nearly exhausted.

"You guys have provided us with the best information anyone has ever given on a UFO sighting. We thank you for that. And so, my last question. Much of this topic is highly classified. That means the public will never, ever learn the truth. You had a front seat last month to the extent that things are distorted and falsified compared to the truth. And we know you did not betray us by telling anyone what you saw. That is really why we are here tonight. We will not take you by force, but my last question to you is this. Would you, all three of you, consider joining our efforts, not as junior members but as full-fledged investigators? We have recruited thousands of junior members, but none have shown the promise you three have displayed.

I don't want an answer now, and don't worry about things like leaving home or how this or that will be accomplished. We will take care of it all. Just think about doing what you have done on a much larger scale, part of an enormous worldwide team of people at least as intelligent as you," John offered.

With that, John shook our hands, the hat spoke into his radio again, and within seconds, they all left. Only Roger looked back with that Hollywood grin and said, "I'll see you soon. Hope you join us."

And we did. Paul and I by the next week and Nancy, brilliant Nancy, only a week later. John was correct. Project Blue Book had an entire system for plugging us into their program while at the same time allowing us to pursue the lives of normal teenagers, then young adults, and finally, where we are now. Of course, Project Blue Book itself officially ended in 1969. It was reported that the program's mission was to actually suppress the legitimacy of UFOs and all things alien. And while that is true, it only explains a small part of what we do.

I cannot even tell you what our organization is called these days, but know that we exist. I am one of the chief investigators concerned with the time travel aspects of unidentified events and craft. Paul now heads one of our west coast divisions investigating underwater phenomena. And Nancy. She works in Houston, Texas, ostensibly for the Veteran's Administration, but actually at a secret underground base, deep underground. Something to do with recovered alien bodies.

Skin

The ship set itself down in a clearing, well inside the boundaries of Area twenty-two.

"Recheck the settings on your skins one more time before we go outside," I said, "And remember, we expect hostilities from the wildlife around here. To them, we are just another food source."

I did my skin check along with the others, making sure all the sensors were up and running and the security and protection systems were at full capacity. After all, we still needed protection from trace radiation, sudden weather changes, and even attacks from some of the species that occupied this new world.

"Comm check, all crew," I ordered after a few minutes. The response was immediate and sequential, just as dictated by our training, and after a few moments, all ten team members had checked in.

After the computer approved the outside air pressure and quality, it opened the door, and we all stepped out. Our mission this week was to oversee the robotic assembly of the four towers, each two hundred feet tall. We were also assigned to do some land clearing and construct a warehouse for future missions. The towers would provide sensor coverage to the area in which the first buildings of Colony One were to be constructed. Our time had finally come.

The fact that the nuclear war started by accident was no coincidence. Too many fingers had poised over too many buttons for too many years. In the end, all the buttons were pressed.

It was much later discovered that the Chinese aircraft carrier had suffered a catastrophic but accidental explosion that most likely originated in its magazine. It was so immense it nearly split the enormous ship in half. The sea did the rest, pouring in through the huge gaps and adding too much weight to the remaining structure. The flagship of the battle group sank within a few minutes, taking nearly all hands with her. A lookout on one of the accompanying destroyers thought he saw a streak of an incoming missile just prior to the explosion and reported it to his ranking officer. Soon after, the word was passed that the battle group was under attack from an American fleet that was practicing wargames nearby. A counterattack was then executed. The American ships responded, and at some point during the exchange, a nuclear-tipped missile was used.

And so, the war began. Things quickly escalated as a rapid response became more important than a pause for negotiation. The nuclear bombardment had lasted several weeks and covered every corner of the earth. By the time it was over, the world had been reduced to a wasteland of destroyed cities, huge swathes of irradiated landscapes, and only small enclaves of survivors scattered across the globe. Some had time to be evacuated to the large and prepared underground shelters and survived the apocalypse. And so, two strains of human survivors started a new evolution: one, exposed to all the horrors of life on the surface of a hostile environment, and the other, a product of life underground, complete with a semblance of its past civilization.

The earth recovered as it always had. Life persisted. It was very difficult at first because of all the negative effects that radiation had on living cells and tissues. But as the years and decades passed, and the radiation levels kept reducing through the various half-lives, things improved. Plant life, insects, and even higher forms like reptiles, mammals, and birds started to reappear. The ecosystem struggled valiantly to find a semblance of symmetry in a very different world, but over hundreds of years, a sort of balance was achieved.

But the cost was high. The radiation had forced many biological adaptations, and most of the creatures that appeared in the new world were very different than those that had lived before. Especially those with relatively short life spans. Thousands of generations of mutated mosquitoes, for example, had resulted in a creature much larger than its ancestors and much more deadly. Many higher life forms had developed poisonous bites to immobilize their prey more rapidly, and in general, all species were much more aggressive.

It was in this world that the surviving and sheltered human civilizations finally emerged from their underground societies. Over three hundred years had passed since the war, but finally, the radiation sensors and atmospheric drones were returning with promising data. Portions of the world had finally recovered enough to where it was deemed "safe" to venture out of the tunnels and caverns that had hosted the organized remnants of a long-gone civilization.

This was the world I was about to head into.

We had done things the right way, trying to anticipate all the needs of a population, from those who actually had lived most of their lives on the surface to those who came many generations later and only knew of life underground. The basics of fresh air, water, food, lighting, temperature control, sanitation, and a myriad of other things were provided. The difference, and what had, in the end, made everything work, was the foresight that humans would have to live and prosper underground for generations and not just a few years, which had been the theory that dominated most scenarios of the past. Manufacturing, agriculture, horticulture, education of all kinds, and even religion were brought underground with the first survivors and have remained through the centuries as companions of the human condition.

Each person was trained extensively in a particular field after completing the basics of high school education. Sloth and criminal activity were not tolerated. Everyone contributed. Technology continued to evolve at a frantic pace and across all dimensions. Over time, a society well-prepared for the venture out to the surface was produced. And when that day finally came, we were ready…or so we thought.

"Mission Base Command, Explorer One, towers up and running. Land clearing operations are underway, with about forty acres now level. Storage warehouse Alpha eighty percent completed," I reported

"Acknowledged, Explorer One. Two days left. How is the schedule?"

"Looks like we are going to make it, Base. Explorer One, out."

Even though internal sensors on all devices had relayed up-to-date data back to our base in real-time, it was still a requirement that I, as Commander of the Explorer One Mission, report every day. As automated and advanced as everything had become, human-to-human contact was still very much desirable.

So far, our week-long assignment has been going well, with only a few minor problems. Abdul had been attacked on day three by a leopard, but the beast had been repelled by his skin defense, an electric shock in this case. And, of course, neither the beast's teeth nor its claws had penetrated the skin. But as expected, the leopard re-attacked twice more before the scaled-up voltage convinced it to give up. Aggressive and predatory insects seemed to be everywhere. From wasps to mosquitoes, some a few inches long, they swarmed our crew but were effectively repelled, again, by our skin defenses. This time by an anti-biological barrier.

It was only yesterday, late in the afternoon, that we made a major discovery, two actually. They were things that all of our advanced technology had missed. I was walking the perimeter of our land-clearing operation when one of my companions, Diana, noticed part of a ruined building mostly buried in the dirt. It had obviously been a human dwelling of some kind and appeared to be from before the war. We were able to enter through an opening on what had been the home's upper level and were amazed to find many items still intact from that period so long ago. Remnants of a bed, a chair, and even an ancient computer lay scattered about the floor.

I noticed Diana pick something up off the floor but, at first, did not pay much attention.

"Commander, look at this," she said as she approached.

In her hand, she held what I remember being called a book. I took it from her and opened it up. Now, from my education, I knew what a book should look like, but this was different. It was not a mass-manufactured product like I knew most books had been, but instead, it was filled with hand-written sentences, some not even finished. I knew enough languages to recognize this as old English but was only able to understand a few words here and there. I could have had my skin computer translate the text, but now was not the time. We had to get back to Explorer One since the night was falling. And since this was our first mission, we were not allowed outside the ship after nightfall.

As we started across the floor toward the opening, part of it collapsed, and Marco fell with the debris through the hole. Diana and I ran close to the edge, careful not to fall in ourselves, and spotted Marco down below. His skin had illuminated in the low light, and our skins modified our sight to make it easy to spot him.

"Are you alright, Marco?" Diana asked, even as her skin showed her that Marco's health readings were all within acceptable levels. Marco's skin had hardened on the outside and thickened prior to his impact below, so there was no physical damage done, but his heart and breathing rates had jumped. He had been surprised and a little scared.

"Yes, I'm okay," he responded, "but I'll need help getting out of here."

"No problem," I said, even as I felt the skin generator between my shoulders activate. Soon after, it made a length of knotted rope in my hands, and with it, Diana and I were able to haul Marco up to where we were. Besides being a little dusty, Marco was fine. After returning the rope material back to the generator, I led the team carefully out of the structure.

But now, we faced another problem. The activity in the house had cost precious time. Night had fallen. Our skins automatically adjusted our vision to infrared and activated our night scan to show us the way back to the ship. But we had been taught about the tenfold increase in the danger from wildlife at night. Hence, the rule was to be on the ship by nightfall. And here we were, about a kilometer away from safety with full darkness upon us.

Already, we could hear strange and wild sounds as we began to make our way back. The terrain itself had been cleared to bare and somewhat compressed dirt. As a result, our exposure was complete, with nowhere to hide or take shelter. And our skins were picking up some inbound movements.

"Explorer One, Commander Davis, do you have our position?"

"Yes, Commander, we have you at point eight five kilometers out at one twenty degrees. Be advised we have a construction grader heading to you now, with an arrival time of under four minutes. But also, be advised, seven contacts look like wild dogs or something similar, heading toward you from the south. They will be on you in less than two minutes. Advise you to huddle and activate max skin defenses. Better do it now, sir."

"Very well. On my signal, have the grader turn on all its lights and the air horn. Hopefully, that will help scare these animals away," I did my best to sound calm.

"Will do, sir. Good luck. Explorer One standing by."

"Okay, guys. Let's huddle up, show these bastards our backs, and go to maximum skin defense. I will signal the grader just before they hit. Diana, give me readouts on their time to impact."

"Yes, sir. Impact in twenty-nine seconds. Seven targets spread out over about six meters. Now twenty-three seconds…"

"Marco, ready?" I signaled.

"Yes, sir. Hope there's enough energy left in the skins for this," he sighed.

"Sixteen seconds, they don't look like dogs, a bit taller. Eleven seconds, now." Diana managed her voice with courage, "Six seconds."

"Okay, guys, this is it!"

We all tightened our grip on each other.

"Activate the grader," I yelled into my skin as Wham! We were hit with the first impact.

A lot happened in a few seconds after that. Though we remained in our huddle, arms wrapped tight around each other, the first and second impacts combined to knock us over off our feet. At the same time, each of us felt our skin defenses activate, sending a high-voltage electric shock into the attackers just as others started landing on us. I felt several pressure points as something tried to penetrate my skin, but nothing did.

At about the same time, the grader, now only about two hundred meters out and coming on strong, turned on both its lights and its air horn. The result was immediate. The attackers, whatever they were, scrambled to get away, clearly not used to such a response from their prey. In a flash, all the weight that had been upon us was lifted. We remained locked in position for a few moments afterward, the air horn blaring loudly through our skins, until finally, I said, "Alright, let's get up."

As we did so, I told Explorer One to turn off the grader's airhorn but keep the lights on. I gave a quick check to Diana and Marco and saw that they were alright. Then, I looked around to search out our fleeing enemy. Just as the grader pulled up, I spotted two of them directly through my infrared vision.

Diana had been right. These things did not run like dogs. They were not even four-legged. They looked like people, human beings! And one of them appeared to be carrying something. A spear, perhaps? I filed this second discovery away for now. I had to get my crew back to the ship.

But damn, something strange just happened. Something that needed to be quickly understood.

The next day, some answers were provided. While Diana, Marco, and I slept, our laboratories, both on Explorer One and at home, had analyzed all the data from our skins, the towers, the grader, and even the new-found book. Those that had attacked us were indeed humans, or at least human-like. It was assumed that they were surface dwellers, most likely descendants of survivors dating all the way back to the war, but no one knew for sure. Anthropology noted several observations: the attackers had moved in a coordinated group, and they had weapons, spears, and perhaps knives of some kind. There was no verbal communication either between them or toward us, and finally, there was no hesitation in their attack, no effort made to see us as anything but an enemy or even prey.

And so, at this time, they were to be considered hostile. The decision to communicate with them and try to establish a peaceful relationship was an established doctrine for us, but more information was needed to start any such process.

The anthropologists also reported that the book we found was some sort of diary. Analysis of the writing showed it to be between one hundred fifty and two hundred years old. It had been translated and managed to give some insight into the hardships of the period, but at the time it was written, much had already been lost. Most of the writing was no more than scrawled gibberish. And there was nothing to link the diary to those we had encountered the night before.

As far as my mission was concerned, it was coming to an end. Our skins had been recharged, and, in a few minutes, we would go back out there to wrap things up. The sixty acres of land clearing would be completed today. The Alpha warehouse was done. The only new development was that we would set up auto-defense systems around the towers and the warehouse against any unwanted intrusions.

The next few missions would also be focused on basic construction and security issues. I was sure that our encounter with the surface dwellers would hurry the efforts to find them and at least study them and their ways. And eventually, plans would be made to seek them out and initiate some sort of controlled contact. That's what it was all about, wasn't it? To get along with each other.

Looks like we got another crack at it.

Henry Oak

Michelle saw her mother coming out of the corner of her eye just as she was finishing her weekly maintenance on Henry's enclosure. She placed the gardening shovel in her apron as she stood up and stepped over the perimeter wall, a wonderful display of paver masonry built by her dad when she was just a baby.

Michelle then walked over to the patio table and sat on one of the chairs. It was a beautiful set up adjacent to the walled garden, a small fifteen by fifteen-foot patio composed of a mix of light to dark gray paver stones, upon which a circular table stood with four chairs and a huge umbrella against the rain and the summer's hot sun. A large storage box had been placed at the end of the patio, and when Michelle noticed that her mom had the lunch basket in her hand, she got up and placed her apron into the box with all the other gardening tools.

"Just in time, mom. I'm starving," Michelle said by way of greeting. Like most girls her age, Michelle seldom ate breakfast, settling for some juice on most days. And so, by mid-morning, she was usually ready to eat something. The basket in her mom's hands looked promising.

"Well, I thought you would be ready for a snack. I brought us a couple of the blueberry muffins from the batch we made last night, along with some skim milk. How does that sound?" Michelle's mom, Becky, smiled at her daughter as she placed the basket on the table. The two of them took a seat on the chairs.

The sky was clear on this late spring morning. In the center of the enclosure, the white oak tree, Henry, provided just enough shade to create a comfortable atmosphere. Becky looked past her daughter and noticed what a good job she had done manicuring the lawn that surrounded the tree. Even the soil inside the immediate area surrounding its trunk was clear of any signs of weeds or clutter. Becky and her husband Lee had discussed the situation last night, and the plan was to bring their fifteen-year-old daughter up to date on the family secret at the next opportunity. And for Becky, the time was now. She waited until the both of them had finished nibbling and sipping and finally spoke,

"Your father and I have decided you are old enough and mature enough to know something about our family. Something you have always been a part of."

"Oh. And what's that?" asked Michelle, leaning forward in her chair.

"Did you ever wonder where the family fortune came from? How are we able to own this magnificent property? After all, it is over a hundred acres in prime Virginia horse country. Or how can we afford for you and your younger brother to be homeschooled by professional tutors? Or the fact that we employ house servants and ranchers to run the horse farm?" Becky asked her daughter.

"Well, sure, but I always thought it was Dad's ability to predict the market, you know, stocks and his other investments," Michelle felt a little excited. She knew she was about to find out something big.

"That's true, but to know the reason behind it all, you need to turn around and tell me what you see," Becky nodded as she looked into her daughter's eyes.

Michelle did just that, but when she looked, all she could see was the enclosure with its grassy lawn, two-foot circle of cleaned soil, and, of course, Henry, the thirty-year-old white oak at its center. She knew that the tree was named after her grandfather, but so what? And she had always wondered why it was so necessary to keep the enclosure around the tree in such pristine condition. There was never anything enforced upon her like the commitment to keep this area perfect.

"What's all this have to do with anything, mom?" She asked. Michelle was curious now.

"This may sound crazy, but bear with me, okay?" Becky had rehearsed this for quite a while, but it still seemed awkward, "Your grandfather Henry was a wizard, a sorcerer, a master of potions and spells, and most importantly, a seer-one who could predict the future," Becky looked steadily into her daughter's eyes as she said these words, and somehow it was communicated to Michelle that as outlandish as it sounded, it was the truth.

"Wow, mom, how can that be?" she said, uncertainty in her voice.

"There are things in this world, even in these modern times, that are secrets. Things known only to a few. Your grandfather was one of those with special powers, and he used them to enrich his family and his friends. He was a good man, one who was himself surprised at his gifts. But he never used them to hurt anyone, only to help. He was even a doctor at one time, a very successful healer. But he soon started to become too well-known, too sought after, so he had to give it up before fame betrayed him," Becky spoke softly.

Michelle was amazed. It seemed like quite a story, and she was a little confused.

"Yeah, but what does it have to do with the tree?" She finally asked.

"The tree is your grandfather, Michelle. Somehow, his spirit lives on in this oak tree," Becky knew this was the hard part.

Either Michelle would accept this or decide they were all nuts. So, Becky continued, "When he knew he was dying, Henry made a deal with the morticians. He arranged to have his body not buried, not cremated but composted. The closed casket at his wake did not contain Henry. Instead, the body was set into a closed chamber with woodchips and plant matter such as straw and alfalfa. In time, bacteria and other microbes broke down the body. It was then heated to destroy any contagion and finally released to your father as mulch. Your dad had been told that the magic that had given Henry his powers would be preserved in the physical remains. It would somehow be extended through to the family, Henry's blood relatives, through whatever grew from the mulch. Lee knew your grandfather loved white oak trees for their strength and majesty. That is why you have an oak behind you now. And why we call it Henry."

Michelle sat back in her chair and stared at her mother. As crazy as it sounded, this tale did explain a lot. Since she had taken over the chore of maintaining the enclosure from her mom, some strange things had happened. She always felt comfortable and somehow protected whenever she was doing the actual work near the tree. There were even a few times when she felt an odd warmth, almost like a caress, surround her on a cooler day.

One time, she thought she saw a person in place of the tree, smiling at her with arms outstretched. And finally, she had thought, on several occasions, that the bark and markings on the tree resembled a smiling face. All had been dismissed as coincidences or her imagination playing tricks on her, but now, there seemed to be more to all those events.

She could not help but think of the bigger picture, too. Her family had never suffered. Never. No one had ever been seriously ill, involved in a serious accident, or suffered a great loss. Her father was well-off enough to spend most of his time at home with the family. Both she and her younger brother Roy were excellent students and masters on horseback. As a family, they had traveled extensively, and all seemed great. Could it be because of Henry that they lived such a "charmed" life?

"Well, it certainly explains why we keep this area so neat and clean. Okay, Mom, I'm in. It does make sense to me; I can believe it. Does Roy know?"

"No, and your father and I think it should stay that way for now, okay? There is a lot more to this, but for now, we just wanted you to know the secret in a general way," Becky was so relieved at how things had turned out, "And of course, not a word, ever, to anyone outside the family, right?"

"You got it, mom. And thanks for telling me. It explains a lot," Michelle nodded.

Becky and Michelle looked up as a horn blasted off in the distance. Lee had just turned off the road and was headed up the driveway toward the house. Both women gathered up the remnants of their brunch, and Becky then grabbed the basket and headed down the gentle slope toward the house.

"I'm going to stay behind for a little while," Michelle told her mom.

"Okay, see you later," replied Becky as she walked off.

Michelle stood by the table for a few minutes, then finally turned to look at Henry. Though she had always done her best with the upkeep, Michelle reaffirmed her commitment to take her best care of this tree and its enclosure.

"Hi, Grandpa," she said with a smile, "now, I know."

Was it her imagination, or did Henry smile back?

Charon's Surprise

New York Times reporter Ron Jarvis held the door open for his guest. Since Dr. Simmons held his briefcase in his right hand, there was no handshaking, but a welcoming smile from Jarvis seemed to be enough. The background check on Dr. Simmons had already been done, so there was no need, at this point, to check credentials. The doctor appeared to match his photograph: forty-five years old with an average build and a round but styled head of brown hair with a matching dense mustache. Jarvis directed Dr. Simmons to a leather chair across from his desk and took his own seat behind it.

"Well, Dr. Simmons, I'm glad to finally meet you in person. Would you care for something to drink or perhaps a light snack before we get started?"

"No, that will not be necessary," replied the Doctor.

"Alright. Since your phone call, we have taken the liberty of checking you out. You are a senior NASA scientist serving as a deputy director of one of NASA's current space exploration missions. That much has been confirmed. But we could only get a hint as to the specifics of the mission. It was something about mapping Jupiter and its moons. I guess that's why you're here, right?"

"That is correct, Mr. Jarvis," Simmons started to say.

"Please, Doctor, just Jarvis, if you don't mind," the reporter interrupted. At six feet, three inches tall, Jarvis had the ability to be both intimidating and as friendly as a big Teddy bear. Today, he elected to present himself as pleasant but not gullible.

"Very well, then, Jarvis," Dr. Simmons continued, "I'm here to tell you a story that holds great implications and significance on a global scale. It is something that goes beyond my secret mission, and it is time-sensitive. I came here because I do not believe in all this government secrecy, and I know you are positioned to get this story out quickly."

"Why the rush, Doctor?" asked Jarvis, "What is so time-sensitive here?"

"Truth is that this mission has been going on for nearly a decade now, and the primary results will be transmitted back to Earth this Friday, only four days from now. And if the story is out by then, the government, through NASA, will not be able to put a lid on it like they have been doing all along," Dr. Simmons explained.

"It sounds like you are risking a lot by coming to me with this story. Aren't you afraid of the repercussions?" Jarvis asked.

"Not really," said Simmons, "I think I will become one of those people that half the country will want to prosecute, and the other half will want to label me as a hero. The result is that they will end up leaving me alone," Dr. Simmons concluded.

"Well, alright then," said Jarvis, "With that out of the way, I am eager to hear the details. Do you mind if I record this conversation?

"Of course not," replied the Doctor.

"Okay, then. Can we start with your secret mission?" Jarvis began.

"No. I think we need to start earlier than that, back to the New Horizon mission. You know the flyby of Pluto that occurred in 2015?" Simmons went on, "I am sure your staff can research all the facts of the mission, so I will only point out the parts that would not appear on any official reports."

Simmons continued, "First, the technology known as optical resolution. We are all fascinated that we can now capture objects in incredible detail from vast distances. The photos from all kinds of cameras are simply amazing in terms of detail and clarity. But it's funny, much of the public has no idea of the true range of optical resolution that we are capable of."

"What do you mean?" Jarvis looked up from his notepad. Even though the conversation was being recorded, he could not help but scribble down words and phrases during the conversation.

"On the New Horizon mission, for example, our closest approach to Pluto was over seven thousand miles, and the closest approach to Pluto's large moon, Charon, was nearly eighteen thousand miles. And yet, the clarity of the pictures of both places showed impressive detail. But that is nothing compared to when the secret photos were shown, the ones that demonstrated our maximum resolution capability. These photos were never revealed to the public for two reasons: one, national security, and two, what those photos revealed. Pluto is barren, though its geology will keep scientists humming for years to come. But Charon holds a tremendous secret. One that confirms the theory that we are not alone in the universe. And one that would also never appear in an unclassified report. This is the true reason I am here today.

Charon hosts a base or did host a base in the past, an alien outpost. The photos reveal a structure, one built many years ago: thousands or millions, we could not tell. It has a geometric shape that could not possibly be natural, a construct of some kind. It's made of some sort of reflective metal. And so, it was determined that we should go back. We were going to send another mission, not to Pluto, but to Charon."

The reporter put his pen down and looked up at his guest. This was much more than he had expected and seemed unreal. When the doctor hesitated, Jarvis simply said, "Go on."

"Okay, alright, where was I?" Dr. Simmons paused for a moment, then picked the story back up, "As challenging as this was, there was much we already knew. To return to Charon, to slow our spacecraft down, to establish an orbit around Charon, and finally, to successfully land at least one rover capable of all the analytical things we wanted it to do. It seemed impossible at first. But then we reviewed what we had been doing over the last eighty years. Especially the rover missions on Mars. And so, it was decided to go ahead with a new and classified mission, the Charon Explorer mission. Jupiter was the cover story.

As you can imagine, the cost of this venture was, itself, astronomical. The government, NASA, and all the involved defense-heavy industries were easily able to hide the funding beyond what was deemed necessary for a mission to Jupiter. But it was another reason to keep the public out of it.

I was placed as one of the deputies in charge of the mission. My job was to oversee the efforts to construct the rover and upgrade its capacities to perform in the environment of Charon, which is much colder than Mars and devoid of any atmosphere at all. New avenues of research were explored new discoveries made, and new technologies developed until, finally, nine years ago, the mission was launched. It was disguised as a mission to Jupiter, and for the most part, very few people had any clue about its true nature.

The surface rover from Charon Explorer has been on the surface of Pluto's moon since last week. It has been approaching the structure for the last few days. It is set to do its initial analysis on Friday and transmit the results to Earth."

"Wow. That is incredible," said Jarvis, "But what proof of all this do you actually have?"

"Well, I have documents here in the briefcase that show the progress on construction of the Charon rover. I also was able to obtain telemetry records of the spacecraft as it flew beyond Jupiter and even several of the Jovian moons. Most revealing of all are closeup pictures of Charon as the Explorer spacecraft approached. I also took the liberty of writing everything down as a report to help your team write the story."

"That is all well and good, Doctor, but if you don't mind, I would like to have my science editor come up here to go over those documents," Jarvis said as Dr. Simmons placed the briefcase on the desk.

"Fine with me," acknowledged Simmons.

Jarvis pressed a button on the large console that occupied the upper left section of the mahogany desk. In mere moments, after a quick knock at the door, a surprisingly young man entered the office.

"Doctor Simmons, this is Darren Williams, our science editor. He has an engineering background and is one of our in-house experts on all things scientific," Jarvis introduced the man.

"Pleased to meet you, Dr. Simmons. I have heard of you," Darren greeted.

"I'm flattered," responded Simmons.

"Now, gentlemen, if we can proceed over to the conference table here, I would like to lay out the documents the good doctor has brought to prove his story and go through them together, one by one."

The scrutiny took over an hour, and there were several questions, especially about the Jupiter telemetry and the photos of Charon. A few others were briefly brought in to focus on the characteristics of the spacecraft. Doctor Simmons responded calmly to all the inquiries and offered great detail in his answers. Finally, Jarvis and young Williams left the room and had their private conversation out in the hallway. For a little while, a bit of doubt started to form in Simmon's mind, but after about fifteen minutes, Jarvis re-entered the office. Williams had gone.

"Well, Doctor, Williams seems convinced that your story is genuine, at least the science part. I am going to take a chance here and approve it. But again, what is the rush? Why can't we wait until the data is in?" Jarvis asked.

"Because, as I said before, twice now, the true data will never be revealed. The real proof will come in on Friday when the details of the rover analysis are received by the Jet Propulsion laboratory. But without some sort of public knowledge of the actual event, all will be denied and kept secret, probably for quite a while before the government decides how to release the information," Dr. Simmons raised his eyes to look at Jarvis, "If ever," he added.

"So, you see, the critical part of all of this is that you print this story, get it out to the public as soon as you can, expose this coverup, and get the truth out. I have been part of NASA for many years, you know this, but the hardest part for me was all the secrecy. There is a culture out there that believes the public should never get all the information, and that sickens me. I am sure it sickens you guys, too," Simmons concluded.

"That it does, Doctor, that it does," agreed Jarvis, getting up from his chair, "I will talk with my editor as soon as possible about this and get this story written. Look for it by tomorrow or Wednesday at the latest. Oh, and by the way, how can I get hold of you for follow-up interviews? I am sure there will be many."

"I am staying at Park Lane until Friday, and here is my card with my phone number on it," said Simmons, "I will probably call you tomorrow to see how all of this is progressing. Thanks for your time. I think we will be making history here," Simmons said.

"I agree," said Jarvis as he came around the desk to see Dr. Simmons out.

The doctor took the elevator down to street level and decided to walk for a while before getting a taxi. After a few blocks, he threw his phony Identification cards into a trash can. He then removed his false mustache and tossed it into the street. He still bore a close resemblance to the real Dr. Simmons, but for today's play, the show was over. He could not believe that he had passed the background check.

That had always been the trickiest part of this whole charade, but it seemed that he got away with it. The documents and photo evidence left from the briefcase were all fakes. The time spent anticipating questions and rehearsing answers also paid off big time.

The only thing left that kept him exposed was the cell phone. He had to allow Jarvis to call him, at least until the story was published. Then, he would toss the phone and be totally free as an architect of one of the biggest hoaxes of all time. He would have his revenge. How dare NASA fire him. And with that, Freddy Casale, also known as Dr. Simmons, hailed a cab, not to the hotel, but to the airport.

Hi Mickey!

Along one of Oregon's many mountainous highways was Stafford's Tire Service, a bustling business that had served the area for over forty years. The current owner, Danny Stafford, had grown up in the business. He had recently inherited it with the passing of his father, Stafford Tire Service's founder and original owner, Daniel Senior.

Since he was familiar with the business, Danny assumed the transition to owner would be easy. For the most part, it was, but there were a few wrinkles. Danny knew that much of his business success was due to its location. Stafford Tire Center was easily accessible from many surrounding towns and cities, with enough property to handle expansion over the years. Other things were also important. His father had always stressed the significance of keeping up with the times and evolving the business to match both changes in the industry and changes in the culture. That was easy to do since, in this area of the country, vehicles of all types traveled the roads, from energy-efficient sub-compact cars to SUVs to massive lumber-carrying trucks. And they all needed tires.

Danny also knew that the most important element in most businesses was the service. That ability to pleasantly deal with customers, all types of them with all types of attitudes, needs, and problems that had to be dealt with. There were those who pretended to know about the tire business and were very suspicious that they were being ripped off to those who put their complete faith in Danny to do the right thing at the right price. Honesty in the business was the most important lesson Daniel Senior had instilled in his son, and it was this element, above all others, that handed Danny the thriving business he now owned.

Danny's father had also stressed the importance of keeping the employees happy. Beyond paying a good salary and providing better than average benefits, it was up to the owners to set the atmosphere around the workplace, to focus on making it a "happy place" where the mood was always upbeat. Daniel Senior believed that granting favors, such as the occasional unscheduled day off or allowing someone to go home a few hours early once in a while, was just part of doing business. Danny understood but did not wholeheartedly agree. He saw it as the workers taking advantage of a good-natured boss.

One example of this was what seemed to be happening with his senior technician. Tommy Eagle Feather was a Native American, one of three working for Stafford Tire. He was an older employee and was said to be a medicine man type of person, someone held in high esteem among the others of his nation. Besides being an excellent employee, Tom had a unique hobby.

He created large carvings out of tree stumps, doing the rough cuts with chainsaws, finishing by using hammers, chisels, and even sanders, and, finally, painting the finished works to perfection. In the past, Tom had asked for and was granted permission by Dan Senior to do this work on company property and to display his pieces along the entrance and exit routes to Stafford Tire. Of course, he would do all this work after business hours and be responsible for keeping everything clean and presentable. As bulky as these carvings were, Tom Eagle Feather did manage to sell a few now and then, and Daniel had always allowed him to keep all the money from such sales.

And so, as one entered or exited Stafford Tire Service, on each side of the driveways, there appeared these enormous painted sculptures, all attached to tree trunk pedestals. A black and white orca stood on its tail, a bald eagle posed ready to fly with wings spread wide, and a huge grizzly bear stood upon its pedestal, arms out and teeth bared. Along with the animals were a few characters from old cartoons. There was a statue of Bugs Bunny, Yosemite Sam, and even Mickey Mouse. There was also a large snapping turtle, a Chinook salmon, and a standing seagull.

This uncommon display turned Stafford Tire Service into somewhat of a tourist attraction over the years. People from all over would pull into the parking lot, sometimes not for tire business, but just to look at the carvings. Danny himself would load up his young daughter, Dana, in her car seat and bring her down to see the statues. She was a bit scared at first, especially of the bear, but in time, she grew to like them all. Her favorite was the Mickey Mouse display because it was a little smaller than the others and very brightly painted. She would cheer up and say,

"Hi, Mickey!" Whenever they first entered the driveway. Fortunately, the parking lot in front of the business was huge and, in most cases, was not overcrowded, even when there were many tourists.

The problem was that Danny started to notice that Tom was becoming less focused on the tire business and more on his hobby. On slow days, he would ask for time off and spend it not by going home early but by working on his carvings. Tom's shop areas did not seem to be as clean at the end of the day as they had always been. And it seemed to take him longer to complete assigned jobs. This was bad enough, but what was worse was that Danny noticed some of the others were slowing down as well. It was time for a talk.

He brought Tom into the office and expected to have a calm and respectful conversation. After all, he was just a kid when Tom started working for his dad. He had known Tom a long time, and though they were never friends, they each managed to get along. It turned out to be a brief meeting.

"I have been here for twenty years, and you are complaining that I am not doing my job?" Tom retorted.

"It's not that, Tom," said Danny, "It seems you are slacking off a bit lately. The others are noticing it, too. Is there anything wrong? Can I help?"

"No, there is nothing you can help me with. It is too late for that anyway," was his reply, "I will step it up going forward, okay?"

"Yeah, sure. I am sure it will all work out," Danny said. He wondered about Tom's "too late" remark but did not push the issue.

Just to follow up, Danny called one of the others from Tom's tribal family, a young employee named Swift Feet. He brought him into the office and asked if he knew of any troubles with Tom. Swift Feet hesitated but then told Danny that Tom had been upset since Danny had taken over the business. Tom thought that he would be given an opportunity to purchase the business from Daniel when he retired, but he was cheated when Daniel died. And any lost opportunity is seen by many of the nation as a loss of pride. Many wanted to take action on Tom Eagle Feather's behalf, but he would not allow it. He decided to live with the shame.

"What kind of action?" Danny asked.

"I cannot say," the young man replied.

Unfortunately, as time went on, things did not get better with Tom. Not only did he fail to "step it up" as promised, but his attitude also changed. His anger started to manifest in ways that were simply bad for business. He started to sound impatient when dealing with his co-workers. He took his lunches by himself. And he even stopped working on his carvings. The last straw was when Tom, after selling one of his sculptures, had arranged for a truck crane to load it onto his customer's flatbed during business hours without asking for permission. As bad as that was, the truck broke down during the maneuver, blocked the driveway, and effectively shut down business for more than three hours.

During the second talk, Danny had to threaten dismissal. He knew of Tom's personal problem but did not mention it. In any case, there was no excuse for what had been going on. Tom apologized for the truck incident and acknowledged that he knew this would be his last chance. Danny held a shred of hope.

But, the very next week, the inevitable occurred. In front of a few coworkers and several other customers, Tom Eagle Feather blew up at a customer who complained he was taking too long to find the problem with her leaky tire. He told her the tire was beyond repair and needed replacement, the same thing he had told her a few days before. Technically, he was right, but by berating her in public like that, he had crossed the line.

Danny ended up apologizing to the lady, outfitting her with four brand new tires and sending Tom to the office.

"I have had it with you. I want you out of here…" Danny was as close to screaming as he had ever been. He took a moment, tried to calm down, and continued, "Tom, I am done here. You have been given several chances, but things kept getting worse. I can't have this anymore. You are fired. You have until, what is today…the sixteenth? The end of the month to get your sculptures and any other personal belongings off the property, but your job here is over."

"I have been cheated," Tom said as he stood to leave.

Danny did not take the bait and stood as Tom left. Danny noticed that Swift Feet and Joey Two Hats left with him. Danny suddenly felt tired and ran his hand through his hair a few times. He poured himself a slug of coffee and drank it down, hot and black. He had a lot of work to do.

After business had closed for the day and the sun had set, Danny remained in his office, thinking about the future of his business. Tom would be hard to replace but not impossible. Toward that end, he had made a few decisions. There were a couple of junior technicians that could step up in the short term. He wanted to wait a while before posting for a new senior technician. First thing tomorrow, an hour or so before opening, he wanted to bring Dana down to see the sculptures again. It always cheered him up when she was happy.

He was just about to leave when he heard a commotion in the parking lot. As he moved to the window to take a look, there was a knock on the door. Opening the door, Danny was surprised to see Tom Eagle Feather standing before him.

"What do you want?" He asked.

"May I come in for a moment?" Tom seemed agitated but more worried than angered.

"Yeah, sure, but what is going on out there?" Danny saw several trucks in the parking lot with people milling about.

"They are with me, but it is not them that is the problem. Please close the door. I need to speak with you," Tom muttered.

Danny did so, and they both sat down.

"Look, if this is about what happened today…" Danny began.

"That is only a small part of it. Please listen to me," Tom said, "As you may know, I am an elder among my people. Not only that, I am also a medicine man, one of a few among the elders. We believe there are both good and evil connections between the worlds of the living, the dead, and those spirits that dwell in us all. But I am not a chief. I can only offer my counsel to those who decide. Do you understand?"

"Yes, but what does that have to do with me? With us?" Danny had no idea where this was going.

"I must confess something. I wanted this business for myself. I saved every day I worked here to have enough money to offer your father a generous sum to buy him out when he retired. I was getting ready to approach him about this just before he died. I loved him and wanted to see him happy in his elder years. Such a tragedy. Anyway, then came you, Danny. I waited because I was sure you would want to sell out and move your family somewhere better. I had doubts that my offer would not be enough for you, and so I waited. But, after a while, I realized that you were going to keep the business. My dream was shattered, and I felt cheated.

Worse than that, however, was that I had told others in my community of my plans. Then we were all in on it, and ownership became a source of pride, not only for me but for all of us. So, when the current situation developed, I was both angered and ashamed. All of us felt that we had been denied something we were rightfully due. Over time, these feelings grew worse and worse. For me, the result was betraying you and the job I have loved for all these years. It was only after you fired me that I realized how wrong I was. I have no malice for you," Tom explained.

Danny started to say, "Well, it's too late for…"

"Apologies?" Tom chuckled in a way without humor, "No, Danny, you got me all wrong. I am not here to apologize. I am here to warn you."

"Warn me. Warn me about what?" Danny suddenly felt an unease, a mixture of anger, fear, and curiosity.

"You have been cursed, Danny. A curse was placed upon you by the chiefs of my nation. This very day. I spoke against it, yelled against it, begged against it, to no end. The only thing I was granted was that the curse is only upon you and not your entire family. You must leave here, stay away for at least two moons…two months, to give me time to undo this injustice. I have risked much just to bring you this warning," Tom said.

Danny almost started to laugh. Surely, this was just some kind of joke or an attempt to scare him into giving Tom his job back. But the look on Tom Eagle Feather's face told him to take this a little more seriously.

"Look, Tom, I appreciate that you came here to warn me and all, but come on! I don't believe in curses or spells or any of that mumbo jumbo. Now take your friends and leave. I am tired and want to go home," Danny sighed.

"Please, Danny, reconsider," Tom tried one more time, "Take your family and go. Get out of here. This is serious business."

"Maybe for you, Tom, but I am not going to dislodge my family on a superstition. Now, get out," Danny said in a resolute tone.

Tom hesitated for a moment, then finally said,

"Okay, Danny, but you have been warned. Your arrogance shall be your downfall, and I wish your spirit well. Beware of those for which you are familiar. They will be your enemies."

"Yeah. Yeah. Now, just go, Tom, alright. Just go," Danny said.

Tom took a long look at Danny, then turned and left. A few minutes later, Danny heard all the trucks as they drove off.

"Man, what a day," he thought as he closed up shop.

The next morning, Danny got up nice and early. He had told Janice, his wife, of his plans with Dana the night before, and she was delighted at the opportunity to get some extra sleep. As quietly as possible, Danny roused Dana, helped with the morning rituals, and soon after, placed her in the car seat for the trip to see the statues.

It wasn't long before Danny pulled into the driveway, and Dana started to sit up and clap her hands as the sculptures came into view. Danny heard her say, "Hi, Mickey," It was truly music to his ears.

Then everything changed.

He heard a thump, and the ground shook. "Earthquake," he thought, "Oh no, not another earthquake."

Then the thump again. And Again. AND AGAIN! He looked in the rearview mirror and stared at an impossibility. The bear, pedestal, and all were hopping to block the driveway! He could no longer back up the car. It was definitely a flight situation, not a fight. But just as Danny went to drive forward, there was a crash on the hood of his car as the eagle, still attached to its pedestal, crushed the engine. His adrenaline level rose off the charts as he felt intense disbelief and panic. To his amazement, he heard, for the last time, his daughter say, "Hi Mickey," as her door was ripped off the car, and Mickey Mouse, now much more than a painted carving, grabbed her car seat and pulled it out of the car.

In more than a panic, Danny took off his seat belt, opened the door, and jumped out. His last thoughts were, "I must save Dana," and, "Why are all these statues chasing me?"

It was the Orca that got him. The giant, wooden killer whale was waiting just ahead in the driveway. Danny, so focused on saving his daughter, did not even notice. The Orca toppled over just as Danny passed in front of the car. He was crushed beneath the monstrous weight and died instantly.

And so, the curse was realized. The spirits that had possessed the statues quickly fled, all but the one in Mickey. It stayed, not for mischief and mayhem, but to protect the child. It had blocked her view of what needed to be done. When the siren sounds of the approaching emergency vehicles broke the peace of the morning, it too flew away.

When the police and the firemen showed up, they found quite a mess. The statues were all out of place. Some were even knocked over and lay on their side. Danny's car was quickly identified, and shortly after, his mangled body was found beneath the whale.

The most extraordinary discovery, however, was the baby girl. Dana was fine. She was found on the ground in her car seat, safe and sound. But oddly, in front of her stood the statue of Mickey Mouse. Its position seemed almost like it was guarding her from the maelstrom that had occurred in the driveway. She was looking at Mickey. And she was happy.

Swimming on Ence

They had eight platforms for the mission after all the negotiations had been completed. By this time, budgetary compromising had once again become a reality. The explorer committee wanted sixteen platforms, and the accountants said they could only afford four. All of them had horse-traded to eight. And that was deemed sufficient by the explorer team.

Each of the lander/submersible craft was attached to the Bus like barnacles on the hull of a ship. The Bus, a large and reusable interplanetary spacecraft, had left lunar orbit only three years ago. With a combination of chemical and nuclear engines, it delivered the Bus crew and the explorer team to Saturn's moon in record time.

The mission was Enceladus, a moon of Saturn. It was essentially a giant snowball, a bright body only three hundred ten miles in diameter. Earlier missions had paved the way to this point, starting with the astounding discovery made by the Cassini probe way back in 2016. At that time, frozen water cryo-volcanoes had been discovered along Enceladus' south pole. The Cassini probe had been reassigned to pass through the ejecta cloud to analyze the composition of the particles that were thought to have originated below the ice and from a global ocean. The analysis discovered the presence of essential-for-life chemicals and even traces of amino acids. As amazing as that was, the true breakthrough occurred when something much larger impacted the sensor array. Cameras aboard were redirected to observe the object, and it was revealed to be some sort of advanced life form, of course, now dead and frozen solid. It resembled a four-tentacled octopus, complete with an eye ridge along its uppermost section. This discovery turned the scientific community on its head, and though efforts to keep things secret were begun, word of the discovery was quickly leaked and became global news.

As a result, there was no hesitation, no lack of either will or funding, to move ahead with follow-up missions. The effort quickly became international, supplanting all kinds of rivalries and even wars between nations. It was an event that managed to link the earth as one world like few things had done.

And so, in 2085, the mission was nearing its focal point. It was the culmination of a frantically paced effort that had resulted from a worldwide effort. The Bus had arrived and settled into orbit around Enceladus, the unmanned probes had been dispatched successfully, and the feedback they provided had cleared the way for the final stage, the human crewed excursion beneath the ice.

"Ready to go for a swim?" Captain and pilot Terry Kunkle glanced over to his copilot.

"I have been ready for the last twenty-five years," replied Lieutenant Sally Ridgewood without looking up from her console.

Only one of the robotic probes had been caught in the updraft whirlpool of escaping water and, therefore, lost to the mission, but its location had been well-recorded, and Kunkle knew to stay clear of the area due south of their location.

"Stand by for submersion," said Kunkle as the Human Probe 1 sank through the last two meters of ice.

"Copy that," was Ridgewood's terse reply.

With a shudder, the HP1 made the transition from ice to water, and the engines instantly converted from heat generation to propulsion. Stabilizer fins popped out along both the vertical and horizontal axis of the craft, and the forward running lights snapped on. The defensive light arrays were also deployed.

The two explorers had studied long and hard on the telemetry transmitted back from the earlier probes to ensure some level of familiarity with the new environment, but both could not help a gasp of amazement when they first saw live the ocean of "Ence," as they had come to call Enceladus.

"HP1 to Bus, we are below the ice and swimming on Ence," transmitted Kunkle, "So far, so good."

"Copy that HP1. Congratulations. Proceed with Track Alpha," The response from the orbiting Bus came through perfectly clear: another hurdle behind them.

"Roger that, Bus. Out here," Kunkle set the submersible onto the preplanned computer-guided program that would take them in a downward spiral. This course would gradually take the HP1 toward what the data suggested was a series of thermal vents, the most likely location for life. The rate of descent would slow as they got closer to the vents since no one was sure yet what, if anything, was down there, nearly a mile below. Pressure sensors would warn them if the squeeze began to get too tight, but the earlier probes had survived, so it was expected that HP1 would be able to complete its mission of discovery as well.

But there were other limits that had to be considered. There were only twelve hours of life support remaining for Kunkle and Ridgewood. Six were needed for the return trip up through the ice and a safe return to the lander, leaving only another six to complete the mission. Of course, there was a reserve of three hours, but no one dared to include that in any calculations.

As the HP1 continued its descent, the view outside began to change. Initially, small particles had been seen floating in the water. When illuminated by the lights, they seemed to float freely past the sub. But now, as the depth increased and the water temperature began to rise, the particles seemed to get larger. And to the delight of both people, there seemed to be independent movement among the particles. They were living things. Though this had been seen before from data of the earlier probes, what happened next was a first.

A larger object, a living example of the quadropus, made its appearance. This was the same creature that had been captured by Cassini some sixty-nine years ago. It came out of the darkness and, with its tentacles, captured several of the smaller creatures. No sooner had one appeared than others started coming in. The sonar sensors started to pick up swishing and crunching sounds as the creatures fed.

"And here it is, Sally. Finally, there is proof of advanced life beyond the earth. This will change everything," Terry marveled.

Terry Kunkle shared a heartfelt smile with his co-pilot as they both witnessed this amazing discovery.

As they continued to watch, more and more of the quadropus creatures arrived in their area, seemingly to feed at will on the smaller life forms. There seemed to be no effort to evade capture. The smaller creatures appeared to not notice the predators among them. The activity continued to increase as the descent continued and the ocean temperature increased. At one point, the collection canister was stretched out from HP1, and several of the quadropus, as well as many of the smaller shrimp-like creatures, were captured and taken aboard as samples. But soon after that occurred, things changed in a dramatic way.

"Warning! Warning! Large object incoming. Distance thirty meters. Impact in twelve seconds. Recommend defensive lighting."

The computer warning was accompanied by a switch from a white light to a red light within the submersible.

"Execute defenses," was Kunkle's instant response.

Immediately, the twenty flexible antennas that extended from all sides of HP1 illuminated a chaotic rhythm of bright lights of all colors.

Simultaneously, the eight high-intensity spotlights illuminated the sea around the craft for a considerable distance. And finally, the sub's active sonar switched on, bombarding the water with a high-pitched noise.

The spotlights along the bow of HP1 caught the creature as it was approaching. It was much larger than the quadropus earlier seen and seemed to have many more arms than its smaller cousins. It had been moving rapidly toward the submersible, intentions unknown, but quickly stopped and then swam off under the barrage of the ship's defenses. As it faded in the distance, both people thought they saw other larger creatures just at the limits of the illumination.

"Let's get out of here, Captain," Ridgewood said in a nervous voice.

"I agree," replied Kunkle. "Release the remote depth probes," he commanded his co-pilot. "Computer, initiate emergency evacuation maneuvers to the extraction point and maintain defenses."

Both of them felt the sudden surge as the computer immediately stopped the downward spiral of HP1 and initiated a direct path sprint maneuver up and toward the ice cover, now quite a distance above. As this was happening, Ridgewood had kept an eye on the backward screen to see what the larger creatures would do in response. She saw that several of them had entered the illuminated zone defined by the spotlights. And in spite of HP1's defenses, still activated, they seemed to be gaining on them.

"Captain, the large creatures are closing on us," she nearly yelled in the tiny compartment.

"Computer, all ahead flank," ordered Kunkle as they both gripped the armrests of their seats to help handle the sudden change in speed. As the sub lurched forward and upward, Ridgewood saw one last thing before the turbulence clouded her view. In a last-ditch effort to capture HP1, the closest of the large creatures shot out a tentacle, much thinner and longer than its others, toward the ship. The tentacle closed rapidly and was just a few meters away. When it finally reached its limit, it went limp and then started to retract. Ridgewood could not help but scream as this action played out so close to their ship.

"Sorry, Terry. That was close," she said with some embarrassment.

"Anymore sign of pursuit?" Kunkle inquired.

"No, sir. Baffles are clear. They must have reached their tolerable limit, perhaps temperature or pressure, I don't know," she replied.

"Very well, Lieutenant. Computer, reduce speed to all ahead full. Secure defensive posture. Continue toward the extraction point. The mission is over," Kunkle ordered.

With that, both crew members were able to relax a little while the computer guided the HP1 to the location where they had entered the ocean. Once they got there, the submersible was reattached to its umbilical. The engines then switched from propulsion to heat generation, and shortly afterward, HP1 started its ascent through the ice channel.

As the ascent was taking place, both Kunkle and Ridgewood had time to reflect on their experience. Both had wished to descend all the way to the seafloor to witness the life forms there. Based upon their actual experience, both assumed that there were many more species as the water temperature increased and the distance to the heat source grew smaller, but that discovery would have to wait for either another expedition or, as long as they received any telemetry from the remote depth probes.

"Chances are, the probes are being eaten or at least torn apart by now," Kunkle said with a snicker.

"Better them than us," laughed Ridgewood in response.

"Well, anyway, we got ourselves some samples. That should keep the scientists busy for a while," Kunkle said.

Ridgewood looked at Kunkle in a strange way, "True, true. Hey, do you suppose those large creatures were somehow the parents of the little ones? And if so, do you think that their attempt to grab us was just because they wanted their kids back?"

Kunkle looked at his co-pilot. Her last two questions seemed so out of character from her normal stone-cold demeanor. But, then again, he did hear her scream.

"I don't know, Sally, but it's too late for that anyway. They might have seen us only as prey. Either way, we are lucky to be alive."

"Copy that," Ridgewood said as they both got back to focusing on their computer displays.

The ascent continued without incident, and the HP1 was recovered to the lander a few hours later. After shutting everything down on the submersible, both were quite relieved to transfer to the slightly roomier lander cabin. Once they ensured all the sensor and computer data was secured and the samples were safely tucked away, Kunkle and Ridgewood launched off Enceladus and, shortly thereafter, rendezvoused with the Bus .

Though not long in duration, this mission was considered a resounding success, and both of the crew of HP1 were showered with praise and admiration. The samples were taken to the bio labs. There, it was quickly determined that the nutritional needs of both the quadropus and the shrimp were very similar to those of Earth ocean creatures and that their chance of surviving in the sample reservoir aboard the Bus was very high. To the delight of everyone, it was expected that the Ence samples would remain alive during the voyage home.

But for Sally Ridgewood, there was a little bit of sadness, too. Even after a few days of celebration, and as the Bus finally left orbit and started its long journey home, she found herself wrestling with doubt. Sally first thought of her children back on Earth, only three years away now. But as she felt herself slipping away into hibernation sleep, Sally could not help but wonder if it was someone else's children now locked away in the sample holding tank.

Uptown Girl

She was good-looking, well-dressed, and smelled nice, as I was soon to discover. We could tell just by looking at her that this young lady had probably never seen any hardship in her entire life. Until now, that is.

Mark and I had been to Manhattan many times before and enjoyed just walking around. A not-so-quick bus ride delivered us from our hometown in New Jersey to the Port Authority terminal on 8th Avenue. From there, we trekked down to Times Square for a few hours of hanging out in what we believed was the center of the universe. There was nothing like the hustle and bustle in and around Times Square on a busy and sunny spring day.

But all jewels have their flaws. And the Times Square area was no exception. All kinds of people visited: tourists like Mark and me, shoppers like this young uptown girl, and even criminals like the two muggers we were just about to meet.

As we passed a small alleyway between a restaurant and a jewelry store, Mark noticed an assault taking place in the shadows. One guy had the young lady up against the wall, yelling in her face as his partner was trying to strip her of her handbag, an outlandish Gucci design, no doubt, that was probably worth more than I made in a month.

We did not hesitate.

"Hey! Cut it out!" I yelled as we both charged down the alley toward the assailants.

Both guys immediately stopped harassing the girl and turned toward us as we closed the distance. The one on my left reached for his back pocket with his right hand. I suspected that he was about to pull a knife or even a gun, so I immediately hit him on the nose with the heel of my right palm. His head snapped back, and a torrent of blood sprang from his nose as he forgot all about what was in his pocket. I then grabbed his right wrist with my left hand, his shirt lapel with my right, and slammed him into the wall. He settled down into a squat.

Mark, in the meantime, had charged into the other guy on the right, the one who had pushed the girl against the building. His head moved to the right to avoid a punch thrown by the mugger, and then quickly, Mark spun him around and applied a chokehold to his neck. After a short time, the mugger slumped down to the ground.

The young girl's reaction surprised both Mark and me. We expected her to start flailing at the two assailants, throwing her own slaps, punches, and even kicks at both while screaming at them. But she did none of that. Instead, she stood very still and alternated a calm and scrutinizing look at both the assailants and the two of us. By now, everyone had come to realize that the fight was over. The two muggers had recovered enough to stand back up and trot out of the darkened alleyway empty-handed, and hopefully, lesson learned. Neither Mark nor I made a move to pursue them. Instead, when the coast was clear, we both turned to the girl.

"Are you alright?" Mark inquired as we both flared our nostrils to catch her perfume.

"Yes, thanks to you guys," she replied, still gazing at us in an uncharacteristically thoughtful way. After a few moments of this, she seemed to make a decision. And then everything went nuts.

Before our eyes, our unbelieving eyes, this small, frail girl changed her shape. She morphed into a huge, hulking figure, still overall female, but now, with an exaggerated bodybuilder physique, a figure over six feet tall. Her clothes expanded with her, but they, too, changed into an outfit much more primal than the items she wore as her other self. Her face had hardened into a warrior's mask but through it all, we saw the same eyes, the same person. From her huge arms, two enormous hands with fingernails that were more eagle claws than human appendages extended out toward us. Before we could move, those hands gripped us both on our outer shoulders. Mark and I, both frozen in shock, cringed as we felt the enormous power of those hands.

No words were spoken, but in our minds, we heard this creature's voice,

"I am a demon of vengeance, a shifter, a slayer of those who prey on the innocent, the helpless, the weak. Those you overwhelmed would have faced a painful and terrible demise had you not interfered. Indeed, all who see me as I truly am meet a horrible fate."

Before we could react, she continued, "But you shall be spared this day. By your actions, you give me faith in the goodness of humanity in spite of all the horrors that people bring to others. Know that you will be remembered by me with kindness and gratitude. When I return to that with which you are familiar, we shall go our separate ways. Speak to no one save each other of me… ever."

Her eyes flashed red as the warning was given, and as we both nodded yes, we were released. The creature seemed then to shrink back down and, within seconds, appeared once again as the polished young lady we had originally encountered.

Mark and I remained still, like two engines that had not started up yet.

"Come on, boys, let's get out of here," the young woman said as if nothing had happened. And with that, she stepped between us, her bag once more over her shoulder, and grabbing Mark and me by the arms, guided us out of the alley and into the light of the street. Then she released us, turned left as we both turned right and walked off, her last words to us, "Have a nice day…"

The Carnival

We were young men, all active-duty US Navy sailors on liberty in southern Italy. My buddies and I had been "on the beach," as liberty is called, for a couple of days now, after our workday ended at 4:00. During the first few days, we had done the typical things, like restaurants, bars, and nightclubs, but word had come to us that a carnival was in town, just on the city's outskirts. So, attending that was the planned activity on this last day before our ship returned to sea.

As we stepped off the gangplank and onto the pier, our cab driver and guide, Carlo, was already there waiting for us. He spoke English well enough to also serve as our translator throughout our times ashore, and we had no problem paying for him and having him join our group for the night's activities. We told him about the carnival, and he agreed to take us there.

After a short but harrowing drive through town, we got to an area with wider roads and more space. Soon after, we saw the fairgrounds. It was set up in a huge farmer's field that must have been between crops and featured a long and wide midway, with many displays bordering both sides. Carlo found a parking spot on the grass near the beginning of the fair, and we piled out.

The midway featured a booth set up on its near end where you could buy a package of coupons that offered discounts for all the attractions at the fair, but according to Carlo, it was a rip-off, so we passed it by. After stopping at one of the food courts and wolfing down some pizza, we set off to walk the midway. One of the first attractions we saw was a unique type of shooting gallery.

"What is this?" I asked Carlo as we approached what looked like a roll of toilet paper on a crossbar with the end extended to the ground, held in place by a bottle of wine. It was only about twenty feet away from the firing line. After a few words with the owner, Carlo replied,

"It is a simple game. You have to shoot through the toilet paper with a BB gun until it breaks, and then you win the bottle of wine. Two dollars for twenty shots."

"Oh, that is easy!" claimed Bowles. He was originally from Wyoming and was supposed to be a crack shot, "me first."

Without too much ceremony, the money was paid, and one of the BB guns, pre-loaded with the twenty BBs, was handed over to Bowles. We all counted as he shot, and sure enough, even before all the twenty shots were used, Bowles had successfully severed the piece of toilet paper held down by the bottle. The owner was a bit surprised and maybe a little angry that he had to pay off after only two dollars was spent, but as it turned out, he was in it for the long game.

We quickly took our prize and sneaked behind the booth area and into part of the darkened field. There, we passed the wine around, each getting a few nice slugs. It tasted rather good, but all too soon, was gone.

"Hey, Bowles, let's get another bottle. That was pretty good," said Crandell. Bowles agreed, and soon enough, we found ourselves back at the booth, counting as Bowles shot. The count was once again right, but after his twenty shots, Bowles had failed to cut the paper all the way through. And so our second bottle cost four dollars. I saw where this was going, so as we were passing the bottle around once again, I made a suggestion, "Well, that was fun. Let's see some of the other things around here."

But Bowles was now angry, "Screw that. I can't believe I didn't get this bottle in the first round. Are you sure it was twenty shots?'

"Yeah, Bowles. No one is trying to cheat you," By now, we all had a little buzz, and my personal alarm told me to take a break from drinking any more wine, at least for now. But Bowles, as stubborn and paranoid as we all knew him to be, pressed on,

"Maybe so, but I am going back one more time." He pushed past me, tossed the now-empty wine bottle to the ground, and walked back to the shooting gallery. The rest of us had a laugh, rolled our eyes, and followed.

This time, the bottle cost Bowles six dollars. It became obvious to all of us what the game was really about, but he refused to accept the fact that his shooting abilities were somehow diminished by the wine. He started ranting and raving that he had been cheated. Carlo was speaking to the owner, trying to calm him down as Murrow, Bowles' closest friend, finally managed to break the spell. Bowles ended up apologizing to the proprietor, and we then escaped the trap.

Further down the lane, we got another lesson. This time at the balloon dartboard. Three darts for a dollar. Each balloon covered a colored dot, and each dot represented either a prize won or a credit toward a prize. After a few dollars spent, we noticed that on some occasions, the dart bounced off the balloon rather than popping it, even after a good hit. Crandell then saw that some of the darts had blunted ends. And after the carny refused to replace a dart for him, Crandell suggested we leave. So, we did.

At one point, we met up with a group of young ladies and, through Carlo, had a good time with them. We took them on the rides with us and spent a while at the various booths. Of course, any prizes we won were given to the girls. A thank-you kiss on the cheek was enough to keep us going, and by the time they said goodnight, all the young ladies had stuffed animals, and our wallets had gotten quite thin, but it was fun, and we didn't mind.

Finally, toward the end of the evening, after more food, go-carts, attempts at things like the Wheel of Fortune, and various mechanical horse races, we found ourselves at the end of the midway. Here, separated from all the other booths, shows, and rides, was something a bit odd. A huge, well-lit sign invited us to board a flying saucer-type ride. Carlo further translated that it would *"take off"* at the stroke of midnight. Besides all the other-worldly displays inside the craft, for an extra five dollars, you would be treated to a flight to outer space. To a flight that would take you all the way out to another world, a truly unique adventure.

And midnight was only a few minutes away!

What a pitch.

We watched as several people took their turn at the entrance and went inside.

It was an offer we had to take. There was no one near the entrance to pay. Instead, there was a machine that accepted the money and, one at a time, allowed you to pass through a metal door. It sure looked authentic. As I waited in line, I suddenly had an urge to go to the bathroom.

"Hey guys, I have to hit the head. Don't leave without me," I said as I took off toward the nearby row of port-o-potties. Carlo must have been thinking the same thing, so as my buddies disappeared into the craft, he and I made our way over to the bathrooms.

After taking care of business, I stepped outside the port-o-potty and ran right into a woman carrying a drink. Our collision was intense enough for her to drop her soda and nearly topple over. I managed to steady the lady and prevent her from falling, but not to prevent her from yelling at me. It was pretty bad, but soon after she started, Carlo came up to us. He and the lady had an exchange, and shortly after, the incident was over. I was given a stern look as she walked off. Carlo and I had a brief laugh and started to head back to join our buddies.

By the time we had moved up the midway and were approaching the ride, a strange thing happened. A series of lights illuminated the craft, and a low humming sound started up. All around, a thin veil of dirt and dust started rising up from beneath the thing.

"Damn it, we missed the ride," I said as we stopped walking and stood to watch. I imagined it was quite a show on the inside, and my friends were enjoying the finale of our carnival adventure. By this time, a crowd had gathered all around us as others took notice of this unique event. The lights then started to spin, first slowly, then faster and faster, until it all looked like a series of straight lines. The humming grew louder, too. Most of the people in the crowd of onlookers stepped back, us too. Some covered their ears against the sound.

Then, incredibly, the ship lifted off the ground. I squinted to see the supporting crane or some device that had to be hoisting it up, but there was no such thing. The craft, this fairgrounds ride, was rising off the ground on its own. It hovered in place about ten feet up in the air and then started off into the sky, continually rising even as it started to fly away. Part of me thought, *"Greatest ride ever!"* even as I started to acknowledge something profound was happening. The saucer kept flying away and, at one point, accelerated rapidly. Within seconds, it disappeared into the night sky.

That was the last time I saw my friends.

There was a confusing period after this event. Some in the crowd screamed and yelled. Even Carlo seemed to forget his English for a while when I tried talking to him. We waited for quite a while, it seemed, but there was no return. When the police finally showed up, Carlo thought it best to get me out of there, and I agreed. He brought me back to my ship with hardly a word between us. But once there, my real ordeal began. I brought Carlo aboard with me to confirm my story that my buddies were now missing. The Officer on Duty took down Carlo's contact information before letting him go. The next day, when Bowles, Murrow, and Crandell failed to report at morning muster, I was suspected of aiding and abetting my three shipmates in their possible desertion. However, the accusations were quickly dismissed when further investigations confirmed that my story was accurate. I was immediately isolated from the rest of the crew and sworn to secrecy. Soon after, I was transferred off my ship to a Navy base back in the United States. From there, I was eventually processed out of the Navy. I received an Honorable Discharge, again, reminded to never speak of the incident, and that was that. I guess they handled the explanations to the families about the disappearance of their loved ones, but I was never told anything about that, nor was I ever sought after by any of their family members.

I was visited over the years a few times by federal marshals to ensure I kept my mouth shut and, therefore, remained free from federal custody. I did manage to stay silent about the whole incident, but I finally reached my breaking point.

My anxiety and frustration have been building for years, and now, I refuse to hold this inside me anymore. I don't know how my story fits into the wide scheme of things or what will happen to me now that I have told it. But I don't care anymore.

Do you hear me? I just don't care.

Acknowledgment

Many people have assisted me in this project in one way or another. My wife, Susan especially, suffered through many rough draft readings en route to the finished product. Feedback on various iterations of these tales was provided by my close friend Arty Casale, a labor he never hesitated to take on, and his efforts, on many occasions, aided me in writing a better story. Finally, my association with the Montclair Write Group has inspired me to pursue my love of writing and has done much to guide me through the experience.

About the Author

Ted Delgrosso was born in Newark, New Jersey, in 1955. He has lived in New Jersey his entire life except for a four-year tour in the Navy that took him all over Europe, the Caribbean, and the Middle East as a Hull Technician. Following the Navy, Ted traveled extensively throughout the United States. He recently retired from a twenty-five-year career at Home Depot.

Ted's Tales Two is his second book, a collection of short stories similar in format to those in his first book, Ted's Tales. He lives in northern New Jersey with his wife, Susan, and their two grown children, David and Diana.

Ted's
Tales

Made in USA - North Chelmsford, MA
49875_9781962624169
12.26.2023 2118